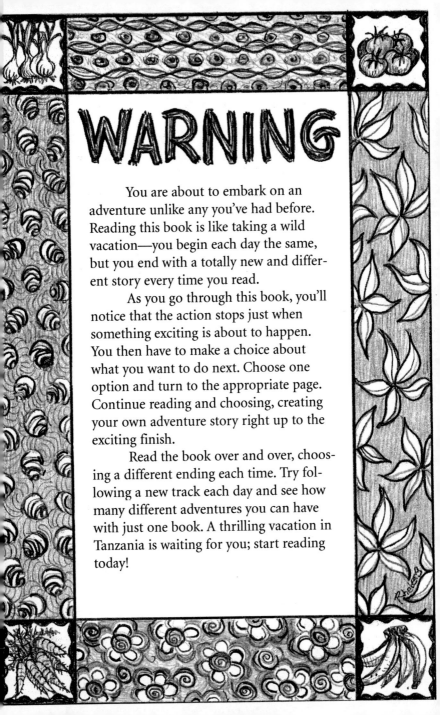

WARNING

You are about to embark on an adventure unlike any you've had before. Reading this book is like taking a wild vacation—you begin each day the same, but you end with a totally new and different story every time you read.

As you go through this book, you'll notice that the action stops just when something exciting is about to happen. You then have to make a choice about what you want to do next. Choose one option and turn to the appropriate page. Continue reading and choosing, creating your own adventure story right up to the exciting finish.

Read the book over and over, choosing a different ending each time. Try following a new track each day and see how many different adventures you can have with just one book. A thrilling vacation in Tanzania is waiting for you; start reading today!

EAST AFRICAN ADVENTURES

The Village Safari

by T.J. Matthews

illustrations by Judy Rheberg

Wycliffe®

Partners in Bible Translation

Orlando, Florida

1-800-WYCLIFFE

www.wycliffe.org

Visit Wycliffe's Web site at *www.wycliffe.org*

You Choose: East African Adventures
The Village Safari
© 2004 Wycliffe Bible Translators
P.O. Box 628200
Orlando, FL 32862-8200

Library of Congress Control Number: 2005017561

ISBN 0-938978-36-5

Printed in the United States of America

To order additional copies of *The Village Safari*, contact Wycliffe's Media Resource Center, 1-800-992-5433, *media_resource_center@wycliffe.org*

Dedicated to Hilda

EAST AFRICAN ADVENTURES

The Hunting Safari

The Canoeing Safari

The Village Safari

ACKNOWLEDGMENTS

I would like to thank Jesus Christ—for saving me by grace, for giving me the opportunity to write and adventures to write about. I would like to thank all the Kahunda missionary kids—Salowitzes, Hamiltons, Luckeys and Milligans, who shared their lives in Kahunda with me.

Mom and Dad, your consistent encouragement is invaluable. Cliff, thank you for being a wonderful brother—you're the reason I can write about siblings who get along and who love each other. To my African friend Hilda—it was your friendship that enabled me to master the language of Kiswahili and that opened the door to East Africa. I look forward to a day in heaven when we can speak to each other freely without any language barriers.

I would like to thank Dorothea Landers, Carol Dowsett, and Pixie Christensen for encouraging me in the early stages of writing. I would like to thank my teachers—Bridget Howard and John and Glenda Leonard—who all worked with me and encouraged me while the books were in progress. I would also like to thank my colleagues Carol Cruzen, Heather Pubols and Judy Rheberg for seeing this project through to its completion.

And finally, *To Him who is able to keep you from falling and to present you before His glorious presence without fault and with great joy—to the only God our Savior be glory, majesty, power and authority, through Jesus Christ our Lord, before all ages, now and forevermore! Amen.* Jude 1:24–25 (NIV)

—T.J. Matthews

PREFACE

Dear Reader,

Once upon a time a family moved from the United States of America to a village in Tanzania called Kahunda. There were two children in this family, a boy and a girl, who spent their early years living out many of the African adventures you are about to read.

As you may have already guessed, I was one of the children in this family. When I eventually left my village home at age 13, I remembered the adventures from my life in Kahunda and from the other missionary kids who lived there at various times. Kahunda is still a part of me, and so I have written the book you are about to read.

–T.J. Matthews

ADVENTURES IN EAST AFRICA

Two of your best friends, Dave and Danielle, moved to Africa about three years ago. You have been emailing them and hearing all about the village where they live in Tanzania where people bathe in Lake Victoria, deal with African wildlife and don't speak English. This summer they have invited you to visit them, and your parents have agreed! As you board the airplane, you look fondly at your familiar surroundings, secretly wondering if you will ever see them again. It's a jungle out there, right? Anything could happen.

After two nine-hour flights with a stop in London in between, your plane lands on a runway in the huge city of Nairobi, Kenya. In the shove of passengers leaving the plane, you spot Dave and Danielle with their parents "Uncle" Darryl and "Aunt" Debbie waiting for you. As you walk to get your luggage through airport hallways packed with people, Danielle, nicknamed Danny, turns to you. "We'll lay over in Nairobi for a couple of days until you get over your jet lag. Then we'll fly out to the village. If you have anything you want to find on the Internet, you'd better do it now 'cause this is your last chance. There are no phone connections in Kahunda where we live."

"Think you'll be ready for it?" Dave asks, with a slightly joking tone. You nod.

A few days later you leave the big city on a small plane with six seats. Before take-off, the pilot makes sure that everyone has a seat belt on and points out the vomit bags. You notice that Uncle Darryl keeps one ready. Dave watches the pilot excitedly all the way through take-off, fascinated by the controls.

In just two hours you arrive in the Mwanza airport, step out of the plane straight onto the tarmac, and carry your luggage from the runway over to the airport's waiting room. In Nairobi, most signs were in English. Here everything is in Kiswahili. Uncle Darryl and Aunt Debbie don't seem to have any trouble making the switch.

As you all sit in the waiting room on comfortable couches drinking bottled sodas, you decide to ask the question that has been on your mind since their family moved to Africa three years ago. "Why did you all move to Africa? I know that you're missionaries, but what exactly do you do?"

Uncle Darryl answers, "We're missionaries with Wycliffe Bible Translators. It's an organization that works with people groups to translate the Bible into languages that don't have it yet. Right now I'm working with five Wazinza translators to translate the book of Genesis into their language."

"Why can't they just use the Kiswahili Bible since that is the national language of Tanzania?" you ask.

Uncle Darryl answers, "Though most of them can speak the national language, the Kiswahili Bible generally doesn't interest them. It's not their *heart* language. But now that Wazinza translators are working to translate the Bible into their language, the Wazinza are very interested."

Aunt Debbie continues, "The Wazinza are a people group scattered west of this area. If you include all the related dialects, the group probably numbers about 250,000 people."

"Hey! The DC-3 is landing!" Dave calls from the door of the waiting room, looking out to the runway. You and Danielle get up to go look.

"Is that the plane we'll be taking to Kahunda?" you ask, surprised. It looks like it could probably hold 20 people.

"No, we'll be taking a six-seater Cessna," Dave informs you. You return your bottles to the refreshment counter and then board your flight to the village.

You fly over the coast of Lake Victoria, looking down at farmland sprinkled with compounds of mud homes situated in groups of three or four. Thirty minutes later the six-seater plane bumps down onto a grassy lakeside strip of land—cleared especially for missionary aircraft—and taxis to a stop. You look at the crowd of people surrounding the plane. Some are smiling; some are frowning. You wonder why they are all staring at you.

"Danny," you say, "these people are looking at me like I'm some kind of space alien; what's up with this?"

"Well, you *are* a space alien to them." She laughs at your puzzled face and explains, "Most of these people have lived in this village and the surrounding ones all their lives. Many have never been to a city. You're a foreigner when you are here. People stare at you just because you're different, and a novelty is always worth looking at."

Uncle Darryl puts the luggage in the truck. After a two-minute drive from the airstrip, you arrive at their compression-brick house. "The bricks are made of cement and termite sand," Dave tells you. Lake Victoria starts about 40 feet from the house and stretches out as far away as you can see.

The house has two roofs: a grass one that is built about two feet over a metal one. "The grass roof keeps the house cool in hot weather and dampens the loud sound of rain beating on metal," Danielle explains. "When it rains on the metal roof at church, you can't hear anything, not even the speaker!"

"Kiddos," Uncle Darryl breaks in, "today is the day of the local *soko*, that is—market. It's 1:00, so it's probably still going on. I think your guest would find an African *soko* to be an interesting experience. Also, remember there's a wedding this afternoon. The invitation specifically invited your mother and me, but I'm sure you kids would be welcome."

"You can also stay home today and unpack from the trip if you'd rather," Aunt Debbie suggests.

(Go to page 6.)

"It looks like we have two choices for the afternoon—a wedding or the market," Dave is thinking.

"*Three* choices, Dave. We can just stay home," Danielle reminds him.

"Stay home?" Dave flops backward onto the couch. "Boring."

"Oh, come on, Dave," Danielle chimes in. "There are *lots* of things to do around here."

"We are *not* going to play with your dollhouse," Dave states firmly.

"Honestly, Dave!" Danielle agrees and Dave looks vindicated, but she continues, "Three people can't play with a dollhouse at once! At least not mine. But the little house that you're building out in the yard…now that'll do just fine." Danielle turns from Dave and gives you a secret wink.

"Oh, yeah, that." Dave looks pleased and turns his attention to you. "You've got to see it! My African friends and I have been building it for three months.

The last house we built had a flat roof, so it leaked, but this time we sloped the roof so that it'll shed rain. And the last one didn't have any walls either, it was *just* a roof, but this time one of my friends is tying bundles of thatching grass to the walls. It looks really cool; I mean, it's as big as a lot of African houses. What?" He catches the smirk on his sister's face. "Okay, Danny, so your dollhouse is just a smaller rendition of the same thing, but only dolls can go in your house. *Mine* is big enough for real people. You and your friends use it all the time."

"*Mine* has a refrigerator and a swimming pool," says Danielle, still grinning slyly.

"Oh, yeah, I forgot." Dave rolls his eyes and drops the subject.

"Kids," Aunt Debbie comes into the room, stirring something. "You're both expressing your creative interests in different ways. There's no need for competition. We're proud of both of you."

"Well, I did build the swimming pool myself," Danielle adds.

"I guess we could just hang around the house today," Dave declares resignedly. "Mom, what are you making?" He has just noticed the bowl in his mother's arms. He looks inside and wrinkles his nose. "Green frosting?"

"It's the color of new life," Aunt Debbie replies nonchalantly, heading back out to the kitchen.

"And what are we putting this 'new life' on?" Dave follows her eagerly. You watch the conversation through the pass-through in the wall between the kitchen and the *sebule*, or all-purpose living and dining room where you are now standing.

"The plain cakes I brought from Mwanza. They're going to be the wedding cakes for Phineas and Mariamu," Aunt Debbie informs him.

"Wedding cakes?" Dave groans, half surprised, half-disappointed. You and Danielle follow him into the kitchen and see Aunt Debbie beginning to frost a cake in a 9-inch by 13-inch pan.

"It's like this," Aunt Debbie is explaining to Dave. "The family didn't give me enough sugar for the frosting, but they did give me lots of milk and several eggs. I decided to make pudding for the frosting, which takes less sugar and more milk, and I used the pan that we usually cook *mchicha* in, and *voila*! This is the result."

"Gross…." Dave begins. "I mean, you can't taste the *mchicha* in it, can you?"

"*Mchicha* is the green spinach-type stuff that we eat," Danielle explains quickly to you. "Dave hates it."

"No," Aunt Debbie reassures Dave. "It doesn't even smell like it." She adds drops of blue food coloring to a small portion of green pudding in a separate bowl.

"Well, in that case…." Dave rubs his hands together. "Oh, yeah, right." Dave drops his arms. "I can't have any, because it's for a wedding."

"You can if you go to the wedding this afternoon," Aunt Debbie replies. She's squeezing two blue-pudding names, Phineas and Mariamu, one on each of the green-frosted cake tops through a small hole cut out of the corner of a small plastic bag full of blue goop.

"That's a good idea," Danielle says. "After all," she turns to you, "it's a chance for you to experience an African wedding."

"African *church* wedding," Aunt Debbie clarifies.

"But this is *also* your last chance to experience an African marketplace," Dave adds. "Today is market day, and unless we go soon, we'll miss it. It closes down in the early afternoon."

"Well," Aunt Debbie is smoothing the surface of the cake around the letters, "your dad and I are probably going to the wedding, but if you kids would rather go to the market, that's fine with me. The wedding ends late, so we might be leaving you kids to fend for yourselves for supper."

"Or we can stay home and do something here." Danielle turns to you. "What do you want to do?"

(If you want to go to the wedding, go to page 11.)
(If you would like to go to the market, go to page 15.)
(If you would like to stay home, go to page 17.)

"I would like to go to the wedding," you state decisively.

"Good choice!" Aunt Debbie is busy trying to inflate and seal a plastic bag around the top of each cake so that the top of the bag won't stick to the frosting. "It's at times like this that I would really like a cake-carrier," she says, frustrated. "I didn't know about this part of being a missionary!"

"Get ready to go, kids," Uncle Darryl calls from the living room. "We'll be leaving in 20 minutes."

Dave ties up their Rhodesian Ridgeback dog, Simba, with a loosely knotted rope, loose enough that she could free herself easily if someone unknown came into the yard, but tight enough to send the message that she is supposed to stay home. She whines and wrinkles up her forehead, reaching her paw after you as you all walk away.

The bright yellow sunlight peers through the trees above as you stride down the missionaries' long winding driveway through the wilds of undeveloped church land. You all stop long enough to look at a large fish eagle perched 15 feet above your heads in a tree on the right-hand side of the driveway and then keep going. Walking in soft sand is not as easy as it looks. Your feet sink in with every step. You begin to appreciate what an advantage it would be to be a flat-footed camel. Dave reminds you to watch where you're walking. "Cow herds come down our driveway all the time. You don't want to go to a wedding with the smell of cow dung on your shoe."

You take a sharp left, leave the forested driveway, and find yourselves walking down a better-used road. This road has been reinforced with red dirt called *chandalawe*, so the walking gets easier.

"Wait up!" It's Danielle.

"Danny, we're late!" Dave turns around, frustrated.

"I've got sand in my shoe, and besides, Dave, you don't usually enjoy weddings anyway."

"I like the food!" Dave disagrees. "I just don't like sitting for hours in the church."

"We should probably go on ahead," Aunt Debbie says. "You kids can be a little late."

"Okay. Danny, hurry up!" Dave folds his arms. Danielle sits down by the side of the road, takes off her black slip-on shoe, pours out an entire cup of sand, and then slips it back on over her sock. "All set! Let's go."

You continue walking. You turn off the road and ascend a steep road straight up a hillside that plateaus into the village. Directly ahead is a long, one-story building with a metal roof, stretching over a long porch of smooth cement. "That's the clinic," Danielle tells you. Then from behind....

"Meow! Meeeeeow!"

Dave stops in his tracks. "Oh, no."

"Is it...Chiro!" Danielle whirls around and kneels down to greet the furry black cat.

Chiro trots up with a final "Meow?" and purrs loudly, rubbing around Danielle's skirt as Danielle kneels in the dust.

"Where did you come from?" Danielle says, scratching the cat's ears and under her chin. "You've never followed us so far before!"

"How about 'bad cat, bad cat!'" Dave is far less enthusiastic about the cat's arrival.

"Well, if I discipline her, she probably won't let me carry her home."

"Well, Danny, I think that I and our esteemed guest had better hustle." Dave starts away. "Enjoy taking your cat back. See ya."

Danielle looks up. "Our esteemed guest could come with me."

Dave shrugs. "That's true."

(If you would like to continue with Dave to the wedding, go to page 20.)
(If you would like to go with Danielle to take back the cat, go to page 25.)

"I would like to go to the market," you decide.

"Good choice," Dave affirms. "We can do all the other stuff another day anyway."

"Except the wedding," Danielle adds sadly.

"I was just thinking," Dave says, twirling his market bag in his hand, "as long as we're *going* somewhere, we don't have to go to the market. We have *three* bikes! If we took the bicycles out, for example, there are plenty of other places to ride to."

"What?" you and Danielle say in unison.

"Oh, yeah." Danielle catches on. "We could change our minds and ride up to Kahunda Rock, for example." She nods and goes back to packing Band-Aids.

"So, what's Kahunda Rock?" you ask.

"It's a set of three gigantic granite rocks set on three pointed hills at the top of the mountain in the middle of the Kahunda peninsula," Dave explains. "The middle rock, called 'Kahunda Rock,' is the biggest by far. It's really neat up there! You can see for miles. You can also see Lake Victoria on three sides. There are a lot of other big rocks up there too. Some are even climbable."

"Kahunda Rock isn't our only option," Danielle reminds Dave.

"Right," he agrees. "Since we can bike just about anywhere, we could go up and explore the village and the surrounding countryside! I mean, it's not guaranteed that the places we explore on our unknown route will be as interesting as going to Kahunda Rock, but then again, how would we know if we've never been to them?"

(If you would like to bike to Kahunda Rock, go to page 27.)
(If you would still like to go to the market, go to page 33.)
(If you would like to try an exploration trip, go to page 40.)

"Let's just stay around here," you decide. After all, this *is* your first day and it might be nice to get used to the place before going on an expedition.

"So what are we going to *do*?" Dave is getting a bit impatient.

"I have an idea," Aunt Debbie contributes. "It is work, but it might be fun if the three of you did it together."

"What?" Dave and Danielle want to know.

"You know about our *sisimizi* infestation...."

"*Sugar ant* infestation," Danielle quickly translates for you.

Aunt Debbie continues, "We found a sugar ant nest in the flower box on the front porch, but the house is still infested. Lately sugar ants have been coming in through Danielle's window screens. I think the big nest we've been looking for might be located behind that long wall of stacked bricks on the slab *under* her windows."

"Yeah, that does sound like a good place for an ant colony," Dave agrees.

"Well, I was wondering if you kids would be willing to move all those bricks to the woodpile out back?" Aunt Debbie asks.

"All covered in ants?" Dave folds his arms and shakes his head. "No, thanks!"

"They bite!" Danielle interjects. She doesn't seem too enthusiastic.

"Only the soldier *sisimizi* bite," Aunt Debbie clarifies.

"Yeah, and leave welts!" Danielle exclaims.

"It has to be done eventually," Aunt Debbie concludes. "Not necessarily today. It *would* be a challenge; but if I give you some gloves, and I'm right, we might not have to deal with sugar ants anymore."

"Hmmm." This possibility is obviously quite appealing to Dave and Danielle.

"We could work on the Little House," Dave suggests.

"And we could visit Neema," Danielle looks hopefully at you and Dave.

Dave laughs. "You two can, but I'll pass."

"You never want to go," Danielle pouts.

"You and Neema just talk and play games."

"That's what girls around here usually do, Dave," Danielle declares glumly, "when they aren't *working.*"

"Yeah, I know. I just don't feel like visiting your friend Neema right now. Our guest could go with you. Hope you like to play Go Fish," he mumbles in your direction.

"Yeah, you could come with me," Danielle looks hopefully at you. "Playing Old Maid with only two people gets boring after a while. But don't worry, we play other games too, like Blitz, Chinese Checkers, Bridge-It, and stuff—whatever I can explain in Kiswahili. I'm not quite good enough to explain Monopoly yet, but we just started playing Mille Bourne."

"Well, you decide." Dave leaves it up to you. "This is only your first day here. What do you want to do?"

(If you want to do the job that Aunt Debbie suggested, go to page 51.)
(If you want to work on the Little House, go to page 56.)
(If you would like to visit Neema, go to page 62.)

"I'd rather go to the wedding," you decide. "I don't want to miss anything."

"Okay, well, I'll see you guys later." Danielle leaves with the cat.

You and Dave head for the church. As you near the church, the tune of "Jingle Bells" greets you. You look questioningly at Dave. "That's the demo music on their electric keyboard," Dave explains. "They use it for a wedding march. It's kinda funny," he chuckles, "though it does make a better wedding march than 'Here Comes the Bride,' in my opinion. You know, at the last wedding I went to, I was sitting on the aisle. I got the baby powder right in my face! I guess it was an accident, but I actually had to leave the building I was sneezing so hard." You may not be quite sure exactly what Dave is talking about "getting the baby powder in his face," but you know that you'll find out.

You and Dave enter through the side door and sit on the bench against the wall to your left next to

Aunt Debbie and Uncle Darryl. The inside of the church is packed with people. Bright colors and large prints are quite popular. Everyone seems to be in high spirits. You can't see what the benches are like; they are too crowded. This is a big event. Some people appear to have brought their own handmade wooden folding chairs, presumably to be guaranteed something to sit on.

It's clear that you weren't late; the wedding is still being set up. Two women have begun to lay brightly colored pieces of fabric in the aisle. Each one is about 3 feet by 5 feet long. "Those are *kangas*," Aunt Debbie tells you. "They serve as everything from wrap-around skirts to table covers. They will all be given to the bride after the wedding."

The pastor motions for silence and says a prayer. Then the choir sings a song. It is lively and upbeat and very nasal-sounding to your ear. Finally the wedding procession begins. First two small boys come in, carrying a wooden plaque between them. Seven minutes later the two boys, taking tiny, carefully timed steps to "Jingle Bells," have only made it halfway up the aisle. The evangelist, as Dave calls him, runs out to hustle them along.

The next people to enter the church are the groom and the best man. The best man seems reasonably energetic; the groom looks a little sleep-deprived and nervous. Then the bridal processional begins.

First two girls come in with bowls of flower petals. In a perfectly timed dance, consisting of three steps and a sprinkle, they sprinkle flower petals on alternating sides of the *kangas*.

As they reach the front, two bigger girls come in with aerosol cans of spray deodorant that they spray on alternating sides of the aisle in the same dance. Finally two other girls arrive with the baby powder. They do a couple of dance steps and then send a cloud of powder on alternating sides in time with the music as they move up the aisle. There are no electric lights in the building, but in the light shining through the patterned window holes you see the billowing white clouds.

Danielle comes in the side door and quickly sits next to you on the bench. Just then a very important-looking woman enters and starts slowly and confidently up the aisle carrying a bouquet of silk flowers. "That's the maid of honor!" Danielle whispers. "That means the bride is next! They do really elaborate bride dresses here...." Her train of thought breaks off. "Oh, no!" she whispers.

Not the bride, but Simba, is standing in the doorway of the church. Frightened people pull away from the door. Simba sniffs the air, sneezes, and then, locating her family at the front of the church, trots happily up the aisle. Nobody looks more surprised than the groom. The maid of honor looks horrified.

The best man, however, is working hard not to laugh out loud. Uncle Darryl meets Simba halfway down the aisle, grabs her by the collar, and drags her up the aisle and toward the side door. "*Utusemehe*," he says apologetically to the groom as he passes him. Then the best man, who had been chuckling up to this point, really loses it. He doubles over in laughter, only to be elbowed by the groom. That's when some members of the audience begin to laugh.

"I'll probably have to take the dog home," Dave whispers to you and Danielle. "Come with me?"

"Nope." Danielle shakes her head. "I already walked home with the cat."

Uncle Darryl pokes his head back in the door and sharply motions for Dave to come outside. Dave gets up to go.

(If you follow Dave outside to take the dog home, go to page 46.)
(If you would rather stay for the rest of the service, go to page 67.)

"I'll go with Danielle to take the cat back," you decide.

"Well, have fun, y'all. See you later." Dave walks on as Danielle gets up out of the dirt, holding the cat in her arms.

Just then a man, somewhere in his thirties, runs up to the two of you. He begins speaking to Danielle in rapid Kiswahili, slightly out of breath. You can tell that Danielle is asking him to slow down, but soon the message is conveyed and he dashes away.

"I guess we have a little change of plans," she says to you. "This is the *mganga*, excuse me, the *doctor* at the clinic. He said something about a woman having trouble giving birth. I have to get Dad to do a hospital run to Sengerema with the truck. Since I know where the church is, I'll go get him; you take the cat home. See ya." She plops the happily dozing cat into your arms and runs down the road.

The cat gives you a dirty look, as if it were your fault, and then wriggles to get away to follow Danielle.

After figuring out that it isn't possible, she settles down and allows you to carry her. A few paces later she begins to purr, realizing this isn't as bad as she thought it was going to be.

You walk down the steep road from the village, skidding a few times on the loose dirt on the way down, making the cat nervous and squirmy. When you finally reach the bottom of the hill, she settles down into your arms again, still tense and watchfully alert. You continue along the *chandalawe* road parallel with the edge of the church land, trying to hurry. As you near the right-hand turn into the missionaries' driveway, the cat, like a ray of black lightning, suddenly frees herself from your grasp and bolts into the woods, following a narrow path that disappears into the thick woods and trees. You gaze after her and then around, wondering what could have caused her sudden flight. At least she seems to be heading in the direction of home. As a matter of fact, if your sense of direction is right, that path is probably a shortcut home. Then again, if it isn't, the cat stands a better chance of not getting lost.

(If you try to take the shortcut through the brush, go to page 37.)
(If you would rather take the driveway, go to page 44.)

Kahunda Rock sounded like much more fun than a market. "I'd like to go to Kahunda Rock," you tell Dave and Danielle.

"Let's get the bikes!" Dave heads out the front door, pushing Simba back as she tries to get into the house. You follow. The bikes are chained with a combination lock to a post beside the front porch. They have begun to collect cobwebs. "Mom told us that we didn't have to do any schoolwork while you were here if we could get it all done ahead of time, so we haven't had a lot of time to go bike riding in the last couple of weeks," Dave explains. He opens the combination lock, and then you and he set about untangling the three bikes.

"Be gentle on the brake cables of that bike," Dave warns you. "They break." You test the two hand brakes and discover that one of them, the one for the front wheel, is disconnected. "Don't worry," Dave reassures you. "You won't need the front brakes."

The three of you are packing your picnic lunch as Aunt Debbie and Uncle Darryl walk out the door. "Well, bye, kiddos! Have a good afternoon. Don't forget to lock up when you leave," Uncle Darryl reminds you.

"Be home by 5:30," Aunt Debbie adds. "See you later."

About ten minutes after Uncle Darryl and Aunt Debbie leave, you all start your ride to Kahunda Rock. You've brought lunch, sodas and lots of drinking water. It's going to be a long trip.

You leave the shade of the driveway. All of you walk your bikes up the steep road into the village. As the road abruptly plateaus, the village begins. You all mount your bikes and begin riding. You pass Uncle Darryl and Aunt Debbie walking and wave as you go by. You turn right down a road that Dave tells you is Main Street, hang left at a fork and continue pedaling. The road is composed of fine, powdery, yellow sand six inches deep. You pedal up a steady incline. On both sides of the road are many mud-walled houses, usually arranged in groups of three or four around a dirt courtyard. There are cows, bees, banana trees, flowers, and children everywhere. A crowd of about 20 children is running after the three of you, chattering excitedly in an African language.

"What are they saying?" you want to know.

"I have no idea," Danielle pants. "It's not Kiswahili. It's probably Kisukuma. That's most people's mother tongue around here. Kiswahili is just the trade language, but it's the only language I know."

You have been riding uphill for a while now. The children have dispersed. "Dave!" Danielle calls. "I'm getting tired; can we stop for a minute?"

You all pull your bikes under a mango tree and sit drinking water in the shade. Some littler children come out from the houses nearby. They giggle, watching your every move.

"Do you ever get tired of being watched?" you ask Dave and Danielle.

"Do we *ever*," Dave sighs, leaning back against the tree.

"The worst is when boys come up to the house and stare in my bedroom windows." Danielle brushes away a fly. "Things have gotten better since Dad started chasing them off."

"*Shikamo*," says one of the smaller children.

"*Marahaba*," Danielle answers. Soon there is a chorus of greetings flying back and forth.

A few minutes later you get back on your bikes and keep riding up the road. About 20 minutes later, you are sure that you must be nearing the top. Dave and Danielle turn off the road and onto a gray path leading to the right. You are now riding over large flat rocks. Following the path you duck and weave around

them. The plant life has all turned to scrub bushes. There it is! High over the trees you see the hillcrest with the giant rock.

You all pull off the path and stop. It is amazing how quiet the place is without the sounds of bicycles. All you can hear is the sound of the breeze and a noisy goat somewhere far away.

"We'll hide the bicycles and hike the rest of the way," Dave tells you.

After crossing a field of cassava plants, you reach the base of the rocky hill and begin climbing over and around rocks, dodging thorn bushes, pulling yourself higher and higher. When you reach the top, you are standing in a type of rock garden, with many large boulders sticking out of the grassy ground at odd angles. This is a climber's paradise! An amateur climber's paradise, anyway. Dave and Danielle run ahead. "This is the rock that Danny and I have been trying to get up for years!" Dave tells you. He runs at it and jumps. His fingers catch for a moment in a crack partway up the rock, then he slips back down to the ground. You try. This rock looks very small, compared to Kahunda Rock nearby.

"Has anyone ever climbed Kahunda Rock?" you want to know as you approach the immense boulder.

"Not that I know of," Dave says.

You work your way around Kahunda Rock and join Danielle on the other side. There you see the view

Dave was talking about. A stone precipice drops off directly on the other side of Kahunda Rock. From where you stand at the top, you can see the whole peninsula of Kahunda, and beyond that, the lake and the islands.

"You know what would really top off lunch?" Danielle comments. "Fresh mangoes." She waves her hand toward the fields and houses below, sprinkled with big, round leafy trees. "Besides, tree climbing beats rock climbing any day."

"I don't think so," Dave disagrees.

"I think so," Danielle reiterates.

Three mango trees are standing in the middle of the closest cornfield. They are near enough for you to see the orange and green dots that must be fruit.

"So, are we going to get mangoes?" Danielle asks.

"We could, but I personally would rather stay here and climb," Dave says. "*We* can come back here whenever we want, so it's really up to our guest what we do."

(If you would like to stay and go rock climbing, go to page 71.)
(If you would like to go and get some mangoes, go to page 104.)

"I still want to go to the market." You are not dissuaded from your original decision.

"Okay," Dave agrees.

"Well, since we're still going to the market, I'd better give you this." Danielle hands you a 5,000 Tanzanian shilling bill.

"*Five thousand* shillings?"

Danielle shrugs. "That's only about $6, but it will buy anything at the market."

"Anything?" You'll be able to buy anything you want! This shopping trip sounds like it could be a lot of fun.

Danielle continues, "When you see something you want to buy, just tell me, and I'll find out the price for you. There are no price tags on items. You have to ask the person who's selling how much it is; they give you the highest price that they think you might pay, and then you haggle them down to a lower price."

"Danny loves to haggle," Dave tells you, "but she's too softhearted to drive a hard bargain. If you want to get a really good deal, you should ask me."

"Last time I went I got a handcrafted burnt clay pot almost for free!" Danielle pouts.

"Yeah, I know, that's because that lady is a friend of yours," Dave replies, with a tinge of bitterness in his voice. "You're good in the language so you have friends everywhere. All I ever hear is, 'Why can't you speak Kiswahili like your sister?' and of course I say, 'Huh?'"

"You've got friends too, Dave. You play soccer with them!"

"Yeah and baseball. You don't have to talk much to do that."

"You go hunting and fishing with your friends."

"If you talk then, you scare the animals away!" Dave closes the discussion.

"Well, that lady wasn't exactly a friend. I don't even know what her name is. I just ran into her once on the beach and we got acquainted."

A smile appears on Dave's face. "Oh, *that* lady. 'Ran into her' is right."

"Well, yeah," Danielle says sheepishly. She tells you the story. "One time my chicken went down onto the beach by the lake. I ran down to chase it back, because it could be eaten by any number of things—chicken hawks, *kenges*..."

"Those are *monitor lizards*," Dave interjects.

"...dogs, etc.," Danielle finishes. "Well, the lady from the market was walking by carrying a bucket of water on her head and I..."

"...ran into her!" Dave finishes with a flourish.

"So what'd you do then?"

"I took her up to our house and refilled her bucket with our water. She was happy."

"Danielle has such creative ways of getting to know people. I mean, I never would have thought of that." Dave is getting back on his bicycle.

"Oh, yeah, I'm sure the ladies would love to have you running into them." Danielle heads out the door. "Let's go."

You say good-bye to their parents and start your walk to the market with Simba trotting happily beside you. Dave and Danielle take her back home and tie her up. "We took Simba to the market once before," Danielle begins to explain.

"You probably don't want to hear about it," Dave declares decisively.

You all head down to the lake, take a left, and trudge along the sandy shoreline path with trees on one side, a velvety blue lake on the other side, and a cloudless sky overhead. Nature in perfection. Large white birds fly in the sky, and weaverbirds chirp in the trees. As you round a bend in the path, Dave looks purposefully at the ground. You can't see anything but sand. Almost immediately Danielle begins gazing intently at the bushes.

(If you ask what they are looking at, go to page 75.)
(If you look around yourself, go to page 77.)

Shortcut or not, this is bound to be interesting. You start down the path, watching the small imprints of cat paws on the ground. After about 12 feet, they disappear abruptly. The cat must have gone airborne, climbed a tree, or most likely taken a detour; dead leaves litter the ground on either side of the path. You continue following the trail. So far, so good. You'll probably be home in no time. The sun is shining brightly amid the twittering of birds. You leave the shade of the tall, craggy trees and enter a portion of brush composed of scrub trees and tall, dry grasses. The path takes a sharp right. You follow it, knowing that you should probably take the first left turn. Soon the path opens into a fork. You turn left. When you pass a garbage pit on your right with peach cans in it, you know that you're close to home.

You follow the path from the garbage pit into the missionaries' yard, come to a dead stop, and blink three or four times to make sure that what you're seeing is real. Crossing the yard in front of you is an animal from a dream.

The animal is shaped like a three-foot-long hotdog, covered in grayish-brown fur. It has no visible neck; its head makes up the front of its hotdog-shaped body. It has an enormous mouth with shark-like teeth, small eyes above that, and tiny round squirrel ears. Its legs are only four or five inches long. The animal's tail is as long as its body and looks just like that of a lion with a tuft of grayish-brown hair at the end.

Simba's behavior is almost as odd as the animal's appearance. She's sitting by the house watching the animal disinterestedly as it pounces across the yard inchworm-style, hunching its back up in the middle, then leaping forward, making a beeline for Danielle's pet chicken at the other end. Doesn't that dog know her job? "Sic 'em, Simba!!!" you scream.

Simba wakes up suddenly from her stupor and darts after the animal without her usual barking frenzy. Dead silent, she dashes across the yard. You begin to wonder if it's the same dog. All of this seems unreal. Maybe you're dreaming. Maybe this whole trip to Africa is just a dream.

Simba pursues the animal to the edge of the yard, stops short of the brush, and then trots back over to you, wagging her tail, much more Simba-like.

The chicken is still pecking in the corner of the yard when Uncle Darryl jogs into the yard.

He notices you. "Help me pack?" he pants. "I've got to take a woman to Sengerema!"

Woman…Sengerema…the day's events are coming back to you. Inside the house you help Uncle Darryl pack for his trip: a soda, a stack of tortilla-like flour *chapatis*, a candy bar....

As he speeds off in the truck, you think about the strange animal again and wonder what you should do. If you tell Dave, Danielle and Aunt Debbie about it, they might think you're crazy. On the other hand, you're in Africa! Unusual animals are common, right? Maybe the family will be able to tell you what you saw.

(If you keep the memory of the odd animal to yourself, go to page 129.)
(If you tell the family about it, go to page 146.)

"I want to take an unknown route!" you agree with Dave.

"Me too." Danielle's eyes are gleaming. "Who knows what we'll find?"

"Well, at least we all agree on one thing," Dave grins.

"We'd better tie up Simba before we go," Danielle reminds Dave. "She likes chickens, and there are plenty of them in the village."

You get the bikes. Before you leave, Dave adjusts the seat for you and gives you some tips about the bike. "We disconnected the hand brake to the front tire. It was too tempting to grab the wrong brake going down a steep hill. You know what happens if you lock your front tire at a high speed? You and the rest of your bicycle will flip over the handlebars—or at least that's what they say. The back brake handle is the one to your right. Don't use it any more than you absolutely have to. I've had to replace two brake cables on my bike!" Ten minutes later you begin your ride to who-knows-where.

"We should avoid the main roads," Dave advises, as he struggles to keep his balance on the sandy driveway. "Danielle and I have ridden over the main roads a myriad of times. Of course, you haven't," he acknowledges, referring back to you, "but I think we should try for some really out of the way places!" Dave has reassured you that their driveway is the hardest part of trip. Riding through deep finely ground sand that gives and slips is an art form. It's hard to keep your balance and prevent your tires from spinning out of control. Dave warned you about over-using the brakes, but you find it hard to imagine that anyone could overuse brakes in this environment! You've got all you can do to keep moving. The dirt changes from gray to red to yellow as you ride to higher ground. You are going down the village main street. You pass many *dukas*. These are small shops with one large, open window out front. The vendor stands inside the *duka* and brings forward whatever the customer motions to from outside the window counter. You ride around large puddles of water in the center of the road, and see bus tracks leading in one side and out the other. Periodically you see cows drinking from these muddy puddles of water. You also pass many houses. These are usually set up in family compounds: four houses surrounding an area of swept, packed dirt where the meals are cooked and the animals are constantly wandering.

You pass the school. The large open windows in the classrooms leave you wondering how a student could concentrate. Large pine trees planted in rows around the school drop pine needles on the wide dirt paths bordered with rocks.

"Eventually we'll need to turn off the main road," Dave reminds the group from the front of the line.

"This is as good a place as any!" Danielle turns left onto a narrow path going down a hill into a cornfield. You follow her. Dave brakes, turns around and takes the tail end of the procession.

The path through the middle of the cornfield is narrow, hard and bumpy. You skid down the hillside, cornstalks whipping at your arms, wondering where in the world you'll end up. The downward incline indicates that you must be heading for the lake. You are probably at least half a mile away from the water, so there's no imminent danger. You are amazed at your speed. It's time to slow down. You squeeze gently on the brake lever, only to feel a loose, empty sensation. Something is wrong…terribly wrong. The brake cable to your back brakes must have snapped! You are going faster and faster. You round a bend and find yourself almost on top of Danielle. You have a decision to make. The path is too narrow for two bikes.

You could abort your descent by plunging into the cornstalks to the side of the path and avoid a collision with Danielle that way, or you could try to pass around her. Up ahead, you see a large rock; the path divides two ways around the large rock before merging into a single path again on the other side. This might be your opportunity to pass Danielle, and it's coming up fast! You have to decide now.

(If you turn off into the cornstalks, go to page 79.)
(If you try to pass Danielle on the other side of the rock, go to page 98.)

Taking a short cut would be too risky. You have no idea where that path might *really* lead. You turn off the main road and walk briskly down the driveway in the cool of the tall trees. The silence is incredible! All you can hear is the twittering of birds and the sound of your footsteps until...

"Nyack! Nyack, nyack!" "Nyacking" noises echo all around you. Monkeys! They weren't here this morning, but now they surround you. They leap through the trees and cover the road ahead. Some have climbed into the bushes to the side and are making "nyacking" noises at you. One of them, a scrawny little monkey, is lying on the ground. It bares its teeth at you but hasn't moved from its place. It's probably wounded. The monkeys are making threatening noises at you and baring rows of knife-like teeth. You didn't know that monkeys had so many. You start to get nervous.

You could go back to that shortcut. You could walk right on through. You could look for a way to defend yourself.

(If you go back, go to page 37.)
(If you walk straight through, go to page 47.)
(If you look for a way to protect yourself, go to page 54.)
(If you try to help the injured monkey, go to page 60.)

Outside the church, Uncle Darryl grimly hands Simba's collar to Dave. "Take her home. I need to stay and apologize. Tie her up with a double knot before you come back."

"But what if somebody tries to rob the house!" Dave protests. "Last time we tied up the dog, someone cut the window screen and I lost my wallet!"

"Well, now you know better than to leave your stuff on the windowsill. I'm not expecting that to happen again." Uncle Darryl turns abruptly and goes back into the church.

"Okay!" Dave says, exasperated. "It's not like this is *my* fault. Grown-ups take these things so seriously!" He kicks a stone, jerks roughly on Simba's collar, and you all walk down the road in silence.

Dave is in better spirits by the time you return from tying the dog.

(Go to page 181.)

Monkeys are nothing to worry about. You know; you've seen pictures of monkeys in South America. People keep them as pets! You head confidently down the driveway, look back, and see monkeys moving threateningly towards you. So much for South America. You make a mad dash. Like an Olympic runner sprinting to the sound of thunderous applause, you sprint to the echoes of threatening "nyacking." Glancing behind you, you confirm that three large monkeys are pursuing you. They lope after you on all fours, fangs bared. You can't help but wish you *were* in the Olympics right now. Your legs seem to be running on their own. You had no idea that it was possible for a human being to run *this* fast, particularly yourself. Then you get an inspiration. "Simba!" you shriek. "SIMBAAA!"

There is the missionaries' house up ahead, and Simba is bounding toward you. Right toward you. You leap to the side as she passes beside you in a blur of

orange-brown. You hit the ground in a twisted heap and roll over in time to see Simba pursuing three streaks of gray around the corner. From your place on the ground, you hear a delightful sound: the baying of a hound that has treed something. Three somethings, you hope. A black furry creature is purring around your face and licking you with a tongue like sandpaper. "Oh, hi, Chiro." You stand up and she follows you, purring. *Well, Danielle*, you think, *I took the cat home!*

After a few more minutes Uncle Darryl comes jogging around the corner of the driveway. He calls you to help him pack for his trip to Sengerema. He grabs cookies, a couple of bottled sodas, two chocolate bars, and a stack of tortilla-like flour *chapatis* out of the fridge. On his way out the door, he stops for a quick consultation with you. "Debbie and the kids will probably come home soon. See ya." In a whirl of sand under tires he is gone. You sit down on the gritty edge of the cement porch and listen to the bird calls and the wind in the trees. If you had a key, you could go into the house. You realize too late that your feet are placed right in the middle of an ants' nest and you're brushing off the small black ants when Aunt Debbie, Dave, and Danielle appear around the corner of the driveway. The wedding isn't over, but you've all had a long day. You decide to stay home for the rest of day. Later that evening Aunt Debbie calls from the kitchen.

"Dave!" You look up from where you and Danielle are playing chess. Danielle quickly makes her next move.

"What, Mom?" Dave goes to the kitchen.

"What happened to the *chapatis*?"

"I don't know, Mom."

"You don't?"

"No, really! I don't know. Why are you looking at me that way? I didn't eat them." You decide that this is a good time for you to make an appearance in the kitchen.

"Well, if you didn't eat them," Aunt Debbie is saying, "then who...?"

"Uncle Darryl took them," you tell her.

"So much for having tacos for dinner!" Aunt Debbie groans. "Oh, well, I guess that we'll just have taco salad. And thanks to your visit," she looks at you, "I even have lettuce!"

"Lettuce gets sent out to us when planes come," Dave quickly explains to you. "We can't get it any other way."

At about 1:00 in the morning, the car pulls up to the side of the house. You hear Uncle Darryl discussing the trip with Aunt Debbie. The baby did not survive. The mother will recover in time. You all go back to bed. Tomorrow will be another, hopefully better, day.

The End

"Let's move the bricks," you decide.

"Good choice!" Uncle Darryl calls from the other room.

"I warn you," Dave says in his best knight-of-the-round-table voice. "The task is perilous. We will have to drive out and vanquish millions of tiny foes..."

"...that bite," Danielle finishes.

"Oh, yes!" Dave agrees. "But the result will be the annihilation of the intruders forever! We can do it."

"Watch carefully for the ants with the big heads," Danielle warns you, putting on a pair of Aunt Debbie's old rubber kitchen gloves. Being a nurse, Aunt Debbie was also able to supply you and Dave with latex dentist gloves. Danielle is currently in the process of spraying bug spray all over her gloves, especially on the inside.

"Danny, why are you so worried?" Dave asks, putting on his final glove. He takes another latex glove out of the box and begins blowing it up like a balloon.

"Those anty bricks we're going to move are located under *my* bedroom window. I've seen and felt more ants than some people do in a lifetime," Danielle explains.

"I don't think that you've been bothered all that much more than the rest of us," Dave disagrees, tying off the end of the balloon glove, which is now an enormous circular, air-filled palm with fingers sticking out. He continues, "We've all stepped on *sisimizi* in the middle of the night and had them crawl all over our hands when we discovered that several million had moved into the bathroom sink faucet, looking for water...." Now he is speaking for your benefit.

Danielle raises her eyebrows. "But you've never had them in your bed."

"True." Dave is tossing his glove balloon in the air. He catches it by the knot and then reaches over and begins bonking Danielle on the head with it. "You poor thing...."

"Dave," Aunt Debbie speaks from the doorway, "I would appreciate it if you would ask my permission before taking gloves for balloons; our supply is limited, you know."

"Sorry, Mom."

Danielle is now making desperate attempts to capture the balloon that Dave is holding out of her reach. He attempts to toss it to you, but Danielle intercepts it.

"We're leaving. Bye, kids!" Uncle Darryl calls.

"Bye!" you all chorus.

"See you later!" Aunt Debbie calls. "There are leftovers in the fridge. You can have them for dinner!"

"Okay, Mom!" Dave shouts.

Soon you are all ready in your gloves and old clothes to begin moving the bricks. There are over 100 bricks, each about a foot long and half as wide. These are the same bricks the house is made of. They're dry, slightly crumbly and stacked two-bricks wide.

You begin the work, each toting two bricks at a time over to the woodpile. Simba lies down underfoot. You have to step around her as you walk. "Oh, yuck!" Danielle has just picked up a brick. Underneath are two very large banana slugs and dozens of ants. "If only we could figure out what it is about banana slugs that makes ants stay away from them! Ants eat all other bugs."

"Yeah," Dave agrees. "We could make a bundle on ant repellent!"

Just then you feel something large, cold, and slimy under the brick you are holding.

(If this bothers you, go to page 93.)
(If you calmly look to see what it is, go to page 106.)

You look around and spot a stick lying by the side of the road. Out in the wilderness there are a lot of sticks lying around, but this one is unusual. It is about an inch in diameter, and someone has already broken all the twigs off the sides to make it smooth. Dave and Danielle say that cow herders come down their driveway all the time, swatting the cattle with herding sticks, so that's probably how this stick was used. Anything that can intimidate a cow could probably intimidate monkeys. As you stoop, the monkeys advance threateningly. If they can be threatening, so can you. You stand up quickly, raising the stick over your head and growl. The monkeys vanish like lightning, still making "nyacking" noises. Even the wounded monkey has vanished. You continue your trek down the driveway.

Simba barks at your approach, but seeing the stick in your hand, she crouches, waving her tail back and forth. You throw the stick for her to fetch and walk toward the house. Realizing that you don't have a key, you sit down on the cement back porch to wait.

Uncle Darryl comes home at a run, grabs food and is gone with the truck in an instant. The rest of the family comes back minutes later.

You tell Aunt Debbie about the monkeys. "You did the right thing, picking up a stick!" she congratulates you. "African vervet monkeys are very dangerous. Scientists say they were the ones who brought AIDS to Africa."

THE END

"Let's work on the Little House!" you decide.

"That's a good activity," Aunt Debbie agrees. "You kids have fun. Uncle Darryl and I will be leaving for the wedding soon."

You go out the back door and head into the side yard by the driveway. There is the Little House you keep hearing about. The high side of the sloped roof is 6 feet off the ground. The whole thing is about 7 feet square. The house was built from grass and thin wooden poles left over from when Dave and Danielle's family last repaired their own house's grass roof.

"There's something I've just got to show you!" Danielle tells you excitedly once you reach the Little House.

"That wouldn't be the treasure trove, would it?" Dave asks. He is following you and Danielle, carrying a chair from the dinner table.

"Dave, you'll spoil the surprise!"

"How is it going to be a 'secret' treasure trove if you show it to every visitor we have?" Dave stands up on his chair and begins working on the Little House's grass roof.

"This isn't every visitor we have," Danielle counters. "We don't get visitors from our home country very often!" She continues for your benefit. "Last year our pastor came and Mom and Dad really seemed to be encouraged by his visit, but other children don't come very often." Danielle goes around the other side and enters the Little House. You have to duck to get through the door. Inside, the house is dark and cool. There is only one window, a perfectly square opening in the grass wall. The sandy floor is smooth and flat, as if it had been scraped clean with a board.

"Look over there!" Danielle is pointing to a pile of sticks stacked in a corner. "It looks just like a plain old pile of firewood, right? But move the sticks and brush away the dirt underneath, and *voila!*" Danielle brushes at the sand under the pile with her hand. It wipes away to show two boards buried under the sand of the Little House's floor. She lifts one of them to reveal a space 6-inches deep underneath. "We put the pile of firewood on top because the ground sounded hollow whenever anyone stepped over here." More boards form the walls of the treasure trove; the base is a layer of small pebbles packed into the dirt. On top of the rocks are strewn a collection of odds and ends:

marbles, a pocketknife (wrapped in plastic), some hair clips and a kaleidoscope. Danielle quickly replaces the boards. "Don't let anyone know that this is here."

"Do you guys have any more secret hiding places?" you ask.

"Nope," Dave answers but Danielle doesn't respond. You suspect that she may have another of her own hidden away somewhere else.

A few minutes later Simba's barking diverts your attention from your work. Dave takes a flying leap from his chair, trips twice in the grass and grabs hold of Simba's collar as she edges nearer to a group of African children who just entered the yard.

"It's okay, Simba, these are our friends! This dog can be weird sometimes."

Danielle explains quickly, "One of the 'big' or important men down at the Luo fishing camp has two wives. One of the wives has 8 children; the other has 11. Some afternoons the kids come up here to play. We can all speak some Kiswahili, so we can communicate. They speak their first language, Kiluo, among themselves."

Dave lets go of Simba's collar; she lies down and falls back asleep in the grass. The younger children, who look about 4 years old, crowd closer to the older ones, eyeing the dog warily. There are three girls and eight boys.

Quickly they seem to segregate by gender. The girls cluster around Danielle while the boys start working with Dave on the house. One of the children comes up and motions to ask you for your watch. Before you decide how to respond, Danielle's next suggestion distracts you.

"Dave, maybe we could play a group game this time, like Hide and Go Seek, or Sardines, or soccer or something."

"Well." Dave gets off his chair. "We haven't played War in a while. That's a group game."

"It's *also* a strategy game." Danielle nods thoughtfully. "That's a good idea!" They both look to you for approval.

It seems that you've been called upon to make another decision, and this time for 14 people. You're not quite sure what Dave and Danielle's game of War is, but it would give you a chance to play with boys *and* girls. One the other hand, you *could* stay here and play with one group or the other.

(If you want to play War, go to page 142.)
(If you join the boys working on the Little House, go to page 170.)
(If you join the girls, go to page 182.)

You creep forward cautiously. The monkeys continue making angry "nyacking" noises. You speak soothingly to the monkey on the ground as you approach, not wanting to startle it. It bares its teeth menacingly as you get closer. Suddenly the monkey flips over and locks its teeth on your hand under your right thumb. Your shout sends the monkeys, including the wounded one, fleeing into the bushes.

Someone else is coming. Uncle Darryl jogs around the corner. "There you are! Come on back and help me get ready to go!" he pants. He hasn't seen your bleeding hand. You jog after him.

When you get back to the house, you decide that this would be a good time to tell him. "Uncle Darryl, one of the monkeys bit me."

"Bit you?" He turns around and looks at your hand. "Was it sick? Acting funny?"

"It was lying on the ground. It was hurt…." Your voice trails off.

"Was it drooling? Foaming at the mouth?" You don't remember. "Well," Uncle Darryl laughs with relief, "since we'll be paying to charter a plane to take you to Mwanza for immediate rabies shots, I guess that I won't have to drive to Sengerema after all! It's a long and hazardous drive," he clarifies. "The rest of the family will be here very soon, but we need to clean that bite."

Uncle Darryl radios for a plane; Aunt Debbie thoroughly cleans the wound when she gets back. She seems really concerned. Two hours later you and the woman in labor are flown out to Mwanza. You get your first rabies shot upon arrival, and the woman and baby are rushed to intensive care. Both of them survive, and so do you. Needless to say, you've learned a few things about wild animals, monkeys in particular. The pilot enjoyed saving two lives, and you're glad to have played a part too, even if the shots were painful. The Lord definitely works in mysterious ways.

THE END

"I'd like to visit Neema," you tell Danielle. Danielle's wistful look turns to a delighted smile.

"I'm really glad that you decided to come with me!" she tells you later as you are both trudging down the sandy driveway. Each of you has your arms full of games: board games, card games and others. You can't see your feet, so you trip once or twice on roots growing out into the tire ruts.

"I need to teach you a word before we get to Neema's house," Danielle says. "The word is '*shikamo*.'" Danielle has you repeat it a few times before she explains its usage. "*Shikamo* is the word you use around here to greet anyone older than you. You are only allowed to use it once a day with each person you greet. It's very important in this culture. To forget to greet is rude, and to greet someone twice is insulting. I had a really hard time with it when I first got here! Another rule is that girls have to curtsey whenever they greet someone."

"So what does '*shikamo*' mean, anyway?" you probe.

"I grab your feet," Danielle answers. "But don't worry, you never really have to grab anyone's feet. The correct response to '*shikamo*' is '*marahaba*.' That means 'Do it a few times.' It's just something you say as a response."

As you round the final bend of the driveway, you and Danielle come face to face with an African girl about Danielle's age coming from the other direction. She isn't carrying anything but walks straightly and easily, swinging her arms. "Neema!" Danielle drops her games and runs to Neema. You set your load down and follow, only to be met with a rapid discussion in Kiswahili. You can tell by their hand motions alone that they were each on their way to see the other. Danielle introduces you and Neema shakes your hand. She is a bit shy but seems pleased to meet you. You all walk back and pick up the games dropped in the sand and continue on the driveway. Neema begins asking you questions in Kiswahili, and Danielle serves as interpreter, adding her own comments here and there. Neema's first question is: *Where are you from?* She also wants to know how you and Danielle know one another. You tell her, and she begins asking you questions about your home country. *Do you go to school there? Do they speak a lot of English where you come from? Is it anything like here?*

You arrive at Neema's *mji*, or family compound. The *mji* consists of two structures, one wooden house with a metal roof, and one round mud house with a grass roof that serves as the kitchen. The rectangular house is about 6 by 9 feet in size, and each of the buildings is about 7 feet tall. The first order of business is to greet Neema's family. You and Danielle greet a grandmother sitting on the ground in the shade of one of the homes as well as Neema's father and young stepmother. Neema's two little sisters greet you. You are also greeted by the family dog—slender, lop-eared and very friendly. Neema brings a bench out of the kitchen for you to sit on. She's ready to start playing games, but her father has other ideas.

"*Nahitaji kupiga mubuzi*," Neema tells Danielle and then walks away.

"Neema has to go round up all the goats and bring them back to the pen before she can play," Danielle tells you. You sit in silence.

"Why don't we help?" you suggest. It seems pointless to just sit there.

"Okay," Danielle agrees, with a *why-didn't-I-think-of-that* look.

You and Danielle start off in different directions. As one goat runs away, Danielle grabs hold of the rope tied to its back leg. This stops the fleeing goat in no time.

You notice a baby goat at the far end of the yard. It is standing on top of the cement foundation of an unfinished house. The foundation is standing alone, with a narrow set of steps leading up to where the door will be built one day. The little goat doesn't have a rope, probably because it is so small. You creep toward it, trying not to frighten it. It stays where it is. As you near the steps, you hear shouting. You turn around to see a man yelling at you and waving his arms. You have no idea what he's saying.

(If you try to figure out why the man is yelling, go to page 149.)
(If you try to get the goat, go to page 167.)

You stay at the wedding service while Dave goes outside. "Here comes the bride!" Danielle whispers to you excitedly.

The veiled bride steps through the main door of the church in one of the most elaborate and stunning white wedding gowns you have ever seen. She walks slowly to the front, arm in arm with her mother who appears to be helping her every step of the way. No material was spared on that wedding dress, and the bride is probably taking pains not to trip. As they near the front, the mother of the bride releases her daughter's arm and begins to walk even more slowly, while her daughter moves on ahead of her. As the mother drops behind, the groom starts walking forward. The bride had not smiled until this point, but when the groom reaches her, she can't hold back a small smile. She immediately tries to wipe it off her face.

The wedding then proceeds like ones you've seen before including the rings and the vows. There is no kiss at the end, however; instead, the bride and groom lean over to sign a contract. "The groom will have to pay a bride price to the bride's father," Danielle explains. "They sign a contract to make it official." The deafening "Lelelelelelele!" from the women tells you the wedding is complete.

Able to stand up again, you reenter the bright sunshine outside through the side door of the church. The whole wedding took at least three hours. You see the bride and groom standing in the yard of the church by the main door, greeting everyone coming out of the building. The bride does a low curtsey with every handshake and greeting she gives. Her mother is fussing behind her, trying to keep the beautiful white dress out of the red dust.

You watch as the women do the traditional wedding dance in front of the church. It's an endurance competition, to see whether the women in the bride's family or the women in the groom's family can remain dancing the longest. Facing inward, the circle dance is composed of singing, complicated step patterns and shoulder thrusts into the circle.

"We should be heading to the reception now," Danielle tells you. "Mom and Dad are leaving."

"Mom! Dad!" She runs ahead to where her parents are walking. "You don't have to follow the road! That path over there is much shorter."

"We'll follow the adults," Aunt Debbie tells you. "You kids go ahead and go whichever way you want. We'll see you there. Here comes Dave."

Dave comes jogging happily up the road. "Did I miss anything important?"

"They got married!" Danielle replies.

"No, not *important* like that. I mean interesting, fun!"

Danielle turns to you. "Why don't *you* answer that? Dave's ideas of interesting and fun don't always agree with mine."

(Go to page 181.)

You didn't come all the way out to Kahunda Rock to go somewhere else. "I'd rather stick around here," you tell Dave and Danielle.

"Oh, well," Danielle sighs. She runs out and jumps nimbly over the edge of the cliff. Dave remains calm, so you decide that there isn't anything to worry about.

"Come on, you guys!" her voice floats over the edge. You follow and see that the rock cliff holding up Kahunda Rock has a naturally formed level bench seat in its side about 6 feet down. It is about 2 feet across, 6 feet long and perfectly level. A sloping path on the side of the rock leads down to it, making it possible to get in and out without doing it Danielle's way. It's amazing that a bench this perfect could be a natural phenomenon. Of course, God probably had something to do with it. The drop-off below goes down vertically at least 60 feet, with rocks and trees at the bottom.

Dave takes the path down and then waits for you. You join Dave and Danielle.

"I climbed that once," Dave tells you, pointing to the cliff below as you all break out the *chapatis*.

"That?" You look down the precipice.

"Yup!" Dave grins.

"He means," Danielle pops the cap off her soda bottle and hands you the opener, "that he climbed it *over there*." She points to the left. You see that farther down, the granite precipice breaks up into smaller, stacked rocks, creating seams with trees growing out of them. At least there would be things to grab onto.

"Okay, yes, I did climb it down *there*, but a 50-foot vertical climb is nothing to laugh about. Danielle only got halfway."

"I couldn't reach the next handhold!" Danielle protests. "You should try climbing in a dress!" she adds.

"Where the whole village could see me?" Dave is astonished.

You decide to change the subject. "Do you think that Africa will ever start using aluminum cans?"

"As soon as they get recycling centers," Danielle quips.

"And that won't be for a *long* time," Dave adds. "They already recycle everything until it wears out completely: cans, bags, shoes. And when you can't possibly use things anymore, the children make them into toys."

The rest of the day is fun; there are so many things to do. Dave and Danielle show you a rock fort that they have been trying to build with the smaller rocks, and you help them add to that for a while. Dave insists on rolling at least one boulder off the precipice. You all are startled when Dave declares that it is 5:10. You climb down the mountain and speed home. The trip back is easier, since it is all downhill, but you're completely worn out by the time you get back.

THE END

Danielle runs ahead to the wedding reception to find Aunt Debbie, who rushes you back to the house and gives you some Piriton to stop the swelling from the stings. You spend the rest of the day at home resting.

THE END

"What are you guys staring at?" you ask them.

"Yeah, Danny, what *are* you staring at?" Dave snickers from the front of the line, still looking at the ground.

"I am looking at the bushes," Danielle says with irritation.

"Oh," you and Dave say simultaneously. Dave is still staring intently at the ground as he walks along the beach.

"Okay, Dave, what are *you* looking at?" you still want to know.

"Ant footprints, I guess," says Dave with a chuckle.

"It's what we're *not* looking at that counts," Danielle explains.

"All right," Dave announces. "We've passed it."

"And what was *it*?" You are getting frustrated.

"The men's bathing area," Dave says matter-of-factly. "People in this culture expect you to look the other way."

"It does seem like a strange place to take a bath...within long-range sight of the market," Danielle comments.

(Go to page 84.)

As you look from the sand to the bushes, something out in the lake catches your eye. Suddenly you are looking at nature in a different form. This section of the lake includes many large bunches of smooth white rocks a little way out from shore. Standing around those rocks are five naked men of various ages, bathing. Dave and Danielle were looking *away*!

"Why didn't you guys warn me?"

"We didn't?" Dave raises his eyebrows.

"I thought that you already knew!" Danielle exclaims.

"Sorry," Dave adds.

After you pass, you ask, "How come those guys were bathing right back *there*?"

"They want to keep clean and smell nice!" Danielle replies glibly.

"But couldn't they go somewhere a little more private?" you wonder.

"Well," Dave answers seriously, "everyone in the village knows that when they pass that place, they aren't supposed to look. And they don't. Many of them take their baths in the lake too. The *women's* bathing area is down by the airstrip."

"And how would *you* know that?" Danielle asks.

"Common knowledge," Dave replies.

(Go to page 84.)

You swerve off to the right of the path, trying not to veer too sharply, but your back tire slips. The next thing you know, you are lying down on a myriad of sharp, natural spikes of broken plants, staring up at stalks of corn, wondering how the world could have suddenly gotten so silent. Birds are chirping and the setting is almost idyllic or would be if the broken stalks weren't so sharp. The next thing you hear is the rattle of Dave's bicycle speeding by, just beyond your outstretched legs. Then you hear a long sharp skidding of tires on loose dirt and feet running back up the path.

Your legs appear to be tangled in your bike, which is facing up the hill. Somehow you managed to turn it 180 degrees when you fell. You struggle to sit up as Dave comes into view and blink at him as he stands dumbfounded.

"Are you all right? What happened?" Danielle comes up the path, jogging beside her bike. With the aura of a concerned medic, she begins questioning you.

"I heard you go off the path. Are you okay? Did you break any bones? Can you move?"

You are still busy trying to disentangle yourself from the bike. Dave and Danielle heave it away. Besides some bleeding cuts and some back bruises, you seem to be okay. Danielle is getting out her first-aid kit. Dave has begun to examine the bike.

"No brake cable."

"Yup."

"Good thing you stopped yourself so quickly. If you had continued, the increasing velocity would have made such a stall far more dangerous later on."

"He wants to be a pilot," Danielle tells you quickly.

"I see that the cornstalks cushioned your landing," Dave observes.

"Not really." Your back would suggest otherwise.

A large audience of small persons has appeared out of nowhere. They stand around, staring unabashedly and giggling. A couple of the children look slightly worried.

"*Hi ni mahindi ya nani?*" Danielle asks. The children giggle. "*Ya nani?*" she asks again. "I'm asking whose *shamba* this is," she translates for you.

"A *shamba* is an agricultural farm," Dave translates.

A little girl approaches Danielle shyly.

"She says it's her family's *shamba*," Danielle translates again. "Let's go. We might be able to buy the corn you knocked over."

Walking your bikes, you follow the little girl who leads you happily down the path to three houses framing three sides of a dirt living area. A woman wearing a *kanga* wrapped under her armpits is tending a metal pot over a fire. Danielle tells you that the pot is called a *sufuria*. She calls her daughter over to watch the food, while she comes to greet the three of you. Danielle explains the situation and offers to buy the crushed corn ears. By the end of the visit, you have 15 ears of corn: the 7 you knocked over, plus a few extras thrown in as a present. You have also had a cup of tea flavored with lemongrass and sugar. "That was a nice lady," Danielle comments.

"We should visit there more often," Dave agrees.

When you get home, you remember that Aunt Debbie and Uncle Darryl won't be back for a few hours. You decide that it might be fun to roast corn for dinner. Instead of using a campfire, you, Dave and Danielle use a *jiko*, a small, hourglass-shaped hibachi-type charcoal oven. Once it is lit and the charcoal has turned red, you roast your corn on a wire grill set over the top.

As soon as the kernels begin to turn brown, you lift it off with tongs. Once you spread adequate amounts of butter and salt on it, you dig in. You've decided to eat on the front porch and watch the beginning of the sunset over Lake Victoria. After a few moments of energetic chewing, Danielle is eyeing her ear suspiciously. "I think I got a tough one."

"What are you talking about? It's supposed to be tough!" Dave grins, mouth full.

"Maybe we should have boiled it," Danielle suggests.

"Naw. This is fun!" Dave begins chewing as if his life depended on it. You look down at the plate on your lap to discover the cat eagerly licking the melted butter off the dish. She purrs happily and rubs behind your back before moving on to Dave's.

"Okay, I give up." Dave drops his half-eaten ear of corn onto his plate just as the cat leans daintily over the dish to begin the cleaning process. She ducks her head, runs off a short distance, gives Dave a dirty look, and begins to lick the butter off her fur.

"Fryer Cluck can have mine." Danielle tosses her barely-eaten cob to the chicken that has been carefully watching the whole process. It immediately begins picking the corn off the ear without any difficulty at all. It's no wonder. The chicken is swallowing the kernels whole. You give your leftovers to Simba who carries it away to gnaw on it.

"We've still got 12 more!" Dave exclaims, eyeing the row on the counter.

"Mom and Dad will help us finish them," Danielle reassures him.

Uncle Darryl and Aunt Debbie arrive home from the wedding tired but happy. Aunt Debbie is carrying a plastic bag. "Guess what we'll be eating tomorrow?" She dumps out her plastic bag on the table. Seven ears of corn roll out. "Mama Makeja gave them to us!"

"Uh, Mom and Dad..." Danielle starts.

"Yeah..." Dave agrees.

"There's something we need to tell you about...."

THE END

The bathing area behind you, you are walking down a narrow path through tall, broad-leafed bushes. You leave the bushes and enter the fishing village. This small settlement near the market is a bustle of activity, especially since today is market day. About 100 yards ahead you see roofed wooden boats. The first one must have been carrying at least 70 people. "Those are from the big islands," Dave tells you, "like Maisome, Butwa and Izumacheli." The beach is crowded. Along the edge of the beach there are women standing ankle-deep in the lake water; some are washing clothes, some are washing dishes, and some are washing small children. Dave is greeted by three boys, each carrying a bucket of water on his head.

"These fishing families are Luos," Danielle tells you. "In most of the traditional tribes that live around here, carrying water is strictly women's work. The Luos are different." The other residents of the beach are giant storks with dark blue feathers, white heads and long beaks opening into droopy red throats. Most of them stand about 4 feet tall. They seem most interested in the men who are gutting fish. You soon see why. The unwanted fish guts never go to waste.

"Marabou storks," Dave tells you. Besides the storks, many white egrets are wading in the water by the shore. They are fish eaters, Danielle tells you, which makes you wonder why they are ignoring the fields of tiny fish, each about 3 inches long, drying on the beach.

On your left are many rectangular houses. "That's where most of my friends live." Dave points in the direction of a group of about five small houses. "Their dad is a rich ferry boat owner. He has 2 wives and 19 children."

Danielle points to a house with a large cow pen. "That's where the milk lady lives. She boards people's cows in exchange for the milk. She's a refugee from Rwanda. People around here traditionally do not drink milk, but she started a business. Her daughter Esther is about my age, maybe a little older. She is the only person I know who can play soccer with a baby tied to her back. Her mother had twins and Esther was the oldest girl in the family, so of course she had to carry one of the babies around all the time."

You are nearing a wide path leading inland to the outdoor market. The path is wide enough for a car and full of people socializing, laughing, walking. People watch your every move.

You enter the marketplace through rows of banana sellers. No one has tables; all the products and produce are spread out on tarps and pieces of plastic on the ground, except for clothing hung on lines strung between trees. You decide that the market area must cover about an acre. The land is sloped, so from this vantage point you can see all of the market.

Danielle points out the sights for you. "To our left is the jewelry corner. It's mostly costume jewelry but still pretty. Just beyond that is the sugarcane; up from there is the clothing section. Clay pots are in the top left corner of the market, just beyond the shoes— unless you want to buy flip-flops. Those are on the right side of the market. Women's clothing is in the top right-hand quarter. Between that and us are the peanut section and the cooking pots and basins. Directly to our right is the hashish section. It's generally accepted that only men enter that area, so we won't."

"Some people think that missionary kids are sheltered from all vices," Dave comments with a laugh. "Nothing could be further from the truth!"

Danielle continues, pointing to the far right, "There is the potato and tomato section. To get to the tomatoes and potatoes there, you walk through the

'miscellaneous' section of the market. That's stuff like batteries and pens."

"Danny, we'd better start shopping; people are starting to pack up!" Dave observes.

"I guess we'd better prioritize. I want to get a *kanga*, so I'm going to shop the right side of the market."

"I want to buy some sugarcane, and that's on the left. So," they both look at you and Dave continues, "you can shop either side with one of us. Decide quickly, though; the market is closing. Right or left?"

(If you would like to shop the left side of the market with Dave, go to page 123.)
(If you would like to shop the right side of the market with Danielle, go to page 124.)

You spot Uncle Darryl and Aunt Debbie coming up the road with the pastor. Aunt Debbie looks at the sting directly under Dave's eye and makes a suggestion. "I think that you kids should probably go home and treat your stings with vinegar. It neutralizes the poison. And why don't you take all your friends with you?" She surveys all the other children standing around.

"Can do," Danielle quickly agrees. She gives a quick explanation to the children in Kiswahili.

"Danielle, you've got it mixed up!" Dave corrects her Kiswahili. "You just said that you were going to take them to our house to put *damu* on the stings. That means *blood*!"

"I'm trying to say *medicine*! It's a word something like *damu*...."

"*Dawa*," Uncle Darryl helps her out as he and Aunt Debbie leave with the pastor.

"Kiswahili can be so frustrating sometimes!" Danielle laments on the way home.

"Well, you're better at it than I am," Dave reminds her. "That's why I let you do all the talking."

"It's only because I've had Neema to help me," Danielle explains. "She doesn't make fun of me when I make mistakes; a lot of other girls around here do."

When you reach the house, Simba runs up to greet you, frightening two of the smaller children. Danielle hands out cotton wads torn from a roll and soaked in vinegar. It really does help.

One of the smaller children comes up to you shyly and places something in your hand. Two some-things, actually. They are two tiny baby birds. One immediately flutters off your palm. You catch it with your other hand on its way to the ground.

"Hey, let me see." Dave peers over your shoulder and then regards the boy sternly.

After a short conversation with the children, Dave gives up.

"So what is going on?" you ask Dave. You are still holding the two cheeping birds, one of which has perched on your thumb and is staring at you inquisitively as though you were the strangest tree it had ever seen.

"I asked him where he found them. He said, 'Over there.' I told him that we need to put them back and he says that they are a present."

"*Ni mboga,*" one boy adds, motioning to the inside of his mouth.

"He says that the birds are *mboga*. How do I translate that for you?" Dave is thinking. The children are all beginning to say good-bye and wander away.

"*Mboga*!?!"

"*Food*?" Danielle is shocked. "No!" She asks for the birds, and you hand them to her. She allows one to perch on each hand. "We can feed them, and when they're big enough, we'll release them back into the wild!" She is determined.

The cat is now rubbing around Danielle's legs. "Oh, no, you don't." Danielle, still holding the two birds, peers down at her.

"Oh, well. I give up." Dave throws up his hands. The birds begin cheeping again.

You spend the rest of the afternoon creating a bird home in a box with branches for the birds to perch on, a comfortable nest in one corner, and a peanut-butter lid birdbath in the other. You spend the rest of the evening feeding them water through an eyedropper and bread crumbs with tweezers. You take turns holding them. They perch on your fingers and cheep at you.

Uncle Darryl and Aunt Debbie come home later. They have fun holding the birds too but seem to have apprehensions. When Danielle decides to name them Peeper and BJ, their apprehensions become obvious. "Be careful that you don't get too attached to these birds," Uncle Darryl warns. "They may not live long."

"I know," Danielle agrees, giving Peeper an eye-dropper full of water. "At least we're giving them a chance."

"I had no idea what mother birds went through!" Dave exclaims. "These guys eat constantly."

"I know the feeling." Aunt Debbie sits back.

Soon you realize that BJ has stopped eating. He won't drink either. Peeper is still as hungry as ever. The next morning BJ is dead. Peeper dies later that afternoon.

"They needed their mother," Danielle cries as you bury Peeper far out in the yard.

"Or a bird specialist. They were fun while they lasted." Dave shovels dirt on their tiny grave and then gives his sister a thin smile. She returns it. You all walk back to the house.

The End

You drop the brick and back away. Dave walks up and flips the brick over, revealing three slimy banana slugs, now covered in sand, still clinging to the bottom of your brick. Just then you feel a small sharp pain under your latex glove. You look at the glove and discover that at least six ants, two of them with large heads, have crawled inside. As you rip the glove off, you are bitten again. "Ouch!" For tiny animals, the bite is pretty potent.

"You know, Danny, I don't think that our guest is enjoying this activity," Dave says. He discovers two ants inside one of his gloves, pulls it off and tries to brush them away.

"Just our guest?" Danielle is busy brushing banana slugs off a brick that she is preparing to carry to the pile. She sets down the brick hurriedly to brush ants off her arms.

Dave has a suggestion. "We could put this activity off for another time when our esteemed guest isn't here. Besides, there's another activity I've been wanting to do, and the weather today is just right for it."

"Windy and overcast?" Danielle half-asks, half-observes, looking up at the sky.

"Yup!" Dave grins excitedly. "So," he turns to you, "it's up to you; do you want to finish this job, or do something else?"

"What is the something else?" you want to know.

"Would it have anything to do with that kite book you got for Christmas?" Danielle asks.

"So much for secrets; yes," Dave sighs. "There are some pretty cool kites in the book! The Japanese Fighting Kite looked pretty neat."

"You mean the one with the earrings?" Danielle asks.

"Those aren't earrings; those are balancing weights!"

"Tassels," Danielle clarifies.

"Their only purpose is to keep the kite balanced."

"So what do you want to do?" Danielle asks you. "Kites or more bricks? The Bird Kite looked pretty fun too. Supposedly it flaps its wings as it goes up."

"We can still do this job another time," finishes Dave.

(If you want to finish the bricks, go to page 106.)
(If the kites sound better, go to page 130.)

"Dave, let's stop! I want to buy a ring." A personalized gold-washed ring from Africa is just too good to pass up.

"A *ring*?" Dave comes back.

"Yeah, I want that one!" You motion to the one with the first letter of your name on it.

"Your name," Dave nods.

"You want one too?" you ask.

"*Samahani*," says a male voice directly behind you and Dave. You both jump. Dave moves to the side to let the man see the jewelry, only to discover that the man actually wants to talk. After a short discussion with Dave, the man smiles and walks away, happier but acting nervous.

Dave explains, "He said that he was desperate to buy a Bible. I told him that my parents run a small bookstore, so I guess he'll show up to buy one at our house sooner or later. We have some Kiswahili Bibles he could buy. The Kizinza Bible won't be ready for several more years...."

"Ahem!" The jewelry seller clears his throat.

"Oh, yeah." Dave points to the ring you want. "*Shilingi ngapi?*"

After a short discussion with the seller, Dave looks to you uncertainly. "Does 500 shillings sound like an okay price to you? That's about 60 cents."

Remembering that you have *five thousand* shillings on you at that moment, you nod.

"*Mia tano,*" Dave agrees. He pulls a 1,000-shilling bill out of his pocket.

"We probably don't want to break out the 5,000 just yet," Dave clarifies. "It's a lot of money!" The man grumbles slightly at having to make change and then borrows a 100 and two 200s from the other jewelry seller.

"*Ubarikiwe katika arusi yako!*" he calls after you as you walk away. Then he and the other jewelry sellers begin to pack up.

"What did he say?" you ask Dave.

"Blessings on your marriage," Danielle answers. She has appeared on the other side of you and heard the jewelry seller's last remark.

"What?"

"Oh, yeah," Dave laughs. "Earlier, when I asked how much the ring cost, he asked me when my wedding was. He said that ring is a wedding ring. I told him that *you* were the one who wanted to buy it. All the same, I think that he was teasing."

"Well, we should probably go," Danielle says.

You all walk home with your purchase. Neither Danielle nor Dave bought anything, but for *you*, the trip was a success.

THE END

This is it! You pedal hard and then swerve. Danielle slows to pass the rock on the right side. You zoom around the left side and feel your pedal scrape the rock as you go by and burst out in the lead. Tires squeal as Danielle slams on *her* brakes.

"What are you *doing*?"

"Broken cable!" you call as you zoom out of sight down the hill. You see another rock in front of you. Uh, oh. This one reminds you of a ramp to a ski jump. You're going fast enough to make this stunt a sensation. Suddenly you're airborne. The worst part of it is, you just left the cornfield. You are headed straight for someone's house! You land and swerve around the house to find yourself facing a row of banana trees.

Dodging into the biggest gap between them, you are momentarily blinded by a huge banana leaf. Now you are in someone else's yard. You speed by two women cooking and find yourself back on the path, still going downhill. Children playing a game in the path scatter. That was close! You are beginning to realize that dodging Danielle wasn't such a good idea. You should have bailed out when you had the chance! Now you're going too fast. You hear barking behind you. A large dog is pursuing you. Suddenly you are grateful for the speed at which you are traveling.

Chickens crisscross the path in front of you, barely missing your tires, squawking loudly. Suddenly "Why did the chicken cross the road?" doesn't seem like a simple riddle anymore. You really wonder why they thought it essential to run across the path in front of you. You just ran over one. Now the chickens are past. The dog gives up the chase.

You are riding down a steeply sloping path between tall sunflower plants. This path is wider and flatter than the others. Where are you headed now? Soon it opens up in front of you—the blue of Lake Victoria. You are headed for the beach! Women washing clothes look up as you approach. They sound the alarm and clear children out of the way. There could be worse places to end up. Your tire skids and your bike swerves around in the sand and scoots a short distance before falling over. Your race is ended, just a few feet from the lake water.

Surprised exclamations of "Eh! Eh!" bring you back to your senses. Women and children are crowded around you. You start to wiggle out from under the bicycle, and the women help to lift it off you. Two boys immediately stand it up and begin riding it back and forth along the beach. They discover the lack of brakes and report it to the women who shake their heads, signifying that they understand.

You stand shakily to your feet. Dave arrives, out of breath. "Are you all right?"

"I'm fine, I guess."

"Danielle said you didn't have any brakes!" Dave tells you. "We followed your tire tracks here. Danielle got the job of explaining the situation to everyone who saw you go by. You must have had quite a trip!" You nod.

The boys are having a grand time riding your bicycle up and down the beach. A couple more come and pick up Dave's bicycle, but he takes it back.

Danielle finally arrives, accompanied by an African man. They both look relieved to see you safe and well. Danielle introduces the man as Bwana Paulo, one of the translators Uncle Darryl works with. You notice that Danielle is carrying something in a plastic bag hooked over the handlebars of her bike. "I had to buy the chicken you ran over," she explains.

"I can carry that on my bike rack," Dave offers. Danielle hands him the dead parcel.

"Are you all right?" Bwana Paulo asks you in English. You are so surprised you don't understand him at first.

"Yeah, I'm okay. The sand slowed my bike down before I fell."

Bwana Paulo calls to the boys who bring your bike back. He flips the broken brake handle back and forth a few times. "This can be very dangerous." He adds, "Be careful going home."

You all say good-bye to Bwana Paulo and head back up the hill, walking your bikes.

"It wasn't really my fault," you say.

"We know," Dave reassures you.

"I saw you jump that second rock," Danielle tells you. "It was pretty impressive, even if you didn't do it on purpose."

"How did Bwana Paulo learn English?" you want to know.

"Bwana Paulo went to college in England," Danielle explains. "Not many Wazinza have lived in foreign countries, but the few who have work with my dad. The Wazinza language was an unwritten language, but now they are coming up with a writing system and a dictionary. The people were eager to write their language well, so they appointed their best-educated people to work with our dad on Bible translation. Dad helps the work with a computer and by teaching courses on translation," she explains. "But the translating itself is done mostly by the local translators."

"The translators publish other materials too," Dave interjects, "like traditional stories! Their language is really important to them. Whenever something is translated, the translators take it back to committees of elders who pore over it for hours looking for mistakes or ways to improve it. They don't take it lightly."

"Bwana Paulo goes to the Pentecostal church one village over," Danielle tells you. "They just got their copy of a tract of different verses from the Bible that the translators put out, and they're really happy with it. Apparently, their pastor includes a part of it in his sermons now and then."

"That's cool." Dave is watching the path ahead.

"So I guess you guys are pretty excited about what your dad does," you comment.

"Our mom too," Dave adds. "She spends a lot of her time home schooling us and keeping the household going. She also does medical work in the village." You are all walking your bikes up the hill now.

"It's hard, though...." Danielle scrapes her toe. "I'm not thrilled about their work *all* the time."

"Yeah," Dave catches her drift. "It's like this, we want our parents' attention for ourselves, but they also have their work...." He is silent. "They certainly don't neglect us, and they give us lots of attention and time, but sometimes their work feels..."

"...like competition," Danielle finishes, and then both are silent.

On the way home you take care to avoid all steep downhill slopes because of your lack of brakes. It's a long ride. You all arrive home exhausted. Peanut butter and banana sandwiches are dinner that night.

You'll never look at a chase scene in the movies the same way again. People really can get hurt. You're glad that no one got hurt except the chicken that crossed the road.

THE END

"So we just *take* the mangoes?" Dave asks skeptically as you all trudge down the hill.

"Yup," Danielle answers. "You can help yourself to mangoes from trees that are in someone's field. You only have to ask if you take mangoes from a tree growing near someone's house."

"How do you know all this?" Dave asks her.

"My friend Neema told me." Danielle pushes a branch out of her way.

The mango trees were farther away than you thought, but at last you are all crossing the cornfield. Soon you are standing under the dense shade of the three trees. "This one's mine!" Danielle shouts, running to the one on the far left. She jumps for a low branch about an inch and a half in diameter, but it breaks off in her hands and she drops on the ground. "Oh, well." Danielle gets up and tries again. Dave climbs the middle tree and drops two mangoes to the ground. The third tree is full of fruit but no one is climbing it.

(If you climb one of the trees, go to page 114.)
(If you would rather just stay on the ground and collect the mangoes, go to page 161.)

Three banana slugs aren't enough to keep *you* from finishing what you start. You all continue working. You tilt the next brick to check the bottom of it. No slugs this time. Just ants.

Dave suddenly stops in his tracks. "You guys, I have an idea!" He drops his bricks and runs inside.

"What do you think he's doing?" you ask, as you and Danielle walk more bricks over to the woodpile.

"I don't know." Danielle shakes her head. "Dave's ideas can be anything."

When you return, you find Dave on the back porch writing all three of your names at the top of a piece of computer paper placed on the cement.

"So what is this?" Danielle peers over Dave's shoulder.

"I think I've figured out a way to add a competitive edge to this job." Dave turns around and explains. "This is the 'Freaky Creatures' game. We get a point for each significant animal or insect or slug we find under the bricks!"

"I think that we should give an extra point to the person who finds the first one of any type of animal," Danielle adds.

"Sounds good," Dave agrees.

"Put me down for the first banana slug. Plus two points for the two I found," Danielle says.

"And I had three under my brick," you tell him.

"Okay." Dave gives you and Danielle each three tick marks. He then gives himself four.

"Four!" Danielle exclaims. "What did you find?"

"A gecko and a big cockroach," Dave says, putting down the paper and pencil. "I was the first to see both of those, and I get a point for each."

You all go back to carrying bricks. Danielle's side appears to be yielding more bugs. You are working in the middle, and that appears to have the greatest concentration of banana slugs. You already earned six points on those alone. Dave is discussing switching sides until he discovers a home of large beetles on his side and adds eight points to his score. All of you have found spiders. Collectively, you have identified three types, a tiny jumping spider, a flat silver-dollar spider and a giant fat kind. You have all agreed to forbid the use of bug spray on the bricks, because it would interfere with your contest.

You have made it to the third row down, and the number of ants has doubled. You already have many bites on your arms. Danielle puts on an old

sweater to keep the ants off her arms. As she walks over to write down a point for a banana slug she just found, you discover a new type of bug, only this one is over a foot long, less than half an inch wide, and on Danielle's back. It is a millipede. It is black with what look like millions of little red legs all the way down both sides. The legs move in a wave motion as it crawls slowly around on Danielle's back. "Danny!" you call.

"What?" she begins to turn around.

"No, face the porch! It's on your back!"

"What's on my back?" She peers over her shoulder at you. "This isn't a prank, is it?" Then she catches a glimpse of the thing on her back and screams, jumping up and down.

"Danny, don't freak out!" Dave just appeared from around the porch. "I'll get it off. HOLD STILL!" Dave gets a stick and brushes it off. It lands in the sand upside down, millions of legs flailing. It flips over and rushes away as quickly as an animal can with legs that are only a quarter of an inch long. It's heading back toward Danielle's section of the woodpile. Dave picks it up with the stick, walks away and throws it far into the brush at the edge of the property.

Danielle is sitting on the edge of the slab, shaking. She brushes away a tear. "I just hate those things! I stepped on one walking to the bathroom one night…." She shudders. "So who gets the point for the millipede?" she asks, changing the subject slightly.

"I saw it first," you remind her.

"And I guess that we could say that Danielle found it, so I'll give each of you a point." Dave marks them down. "As it stands now, I have 39 points, if you count that little white spider I found; Danielle has 43; and our guest has 41."

You all go back to work. Under the fourth row is a horrendous quantity of ants; thus the number of bugs has decreased. You bring out a hand broom and take turns brushing the ants off the bricks before carrying them out to the woodpile. You find a moth. As you walk over to mark the point, you hear Dave exclaiming that he has found the first lizard.

"Not a gecko, this one is a bona-fide…." Just then Danielle screams and runs. An 8-inch snake slithers away from her work area. Once it is safely out of sight in the brush, you all regroup. Danielle gives herself two points.

"You guys, this just got dangerous." Dave scratches his head worriedly.

"We only have two more layers to go!" Danielle says, disappointed. "Maybe if we just pushed all the remaining bricks onto the ground…."

"Now you're talking!" Dave agrees. "Just think how many ants were in that last row! They must be riding piggyback at this point…."

"Rat!" you call as you push over your section. The rat scurries into the yard. You're amazed that it could live with all those ants!

"I wonder if it was related to the three baby rats I found under my desk," Danielle muses.

You get three points for spotting the first warm-blooded animal. You agree to give Dave an extra point for finding the ant nursery. Two extra points would have tied him with you, and it isn't really a new animal. It is quite interesting, though, to watch all of the ants carrying away the tiny white eggs. You never do find the ant queen. You assume that she must be somewhere around the nursery but then give up looking for her. She's too well-hidden. Perhaps she is under the foundation of the house itself.

You all carry the last remaining bricks to the brick pile. Then, in a final ceremony, you sweep all the brick dust off the slab and spray the area with bug spray, killing all of the ants that dared to remain.

That evening Aunt Debbie and Uncle Darryl return to find all three of you showered and slumped exhausted on the couch.

"We saw the slab and the brick pile; you kids did a good job!" Uncle Darryl says as he enters the living room. You all smile weakly. "So, was it the 'big colony?'" You all nod.

"Good!" Aunt Debbie claps her hands. "What did I tell you?" she congratulates herself. "Well, I must say, it'll be nice not to have to deal with that any-more!" This time you all nod more vigorously. "So, was it as hard as you thought it was going to be?" she asks, going into the kitchen. You, Dave and Danielle give each other a look before answering.

Later, after your return to your own country, Aunt Debbie writes to you about their new cure for ant colonies: tick powder! "You just sprinkle some tick powder on the nest and the ants carry it to their queen," Aunt Debbie emails. "The queen eats it and dies of poisoning!"

You're proud of the way you helped, even though there was an easier way. At least Danielle doesn't have so much wildlife living so close to her bedroom anymore.

THE END

You run frantically down the road. You've got to get away from these bees. You feel two sharp stings. Dave and Danielle and the children who were with you are following, shrieking. The bees begin to scatter. You swat at one particularly determined bee and then turn around to see what everyone else is doing. Danielle is carrying a crying little boy. He must have tripped while he was running. Dave and two bigger boys are comparing sting marks. One boy appears to have gotten a bee in his shirt, and two friends are helping him get it out. He finally shakes it out of his shirt, stomps on it twice with a bare foot and then swaggers away confidently. Almost everyone has been stung.

(If you are allergic to bees, go to page 74.)
(If you are not allergic to bees, go to page 89.)

You attempt to climb the final mango tree. You walk around behind it to find a place to climb into the first huge fork of the tree's branches. Once you get there, you discover that mango trees are easy to climb. The bark is smooth and there are lots of branches to step on. Large, sun-ripened mangoes are clustered in the outside branches. You keep climbing until you reach the top branch, and then you discover that this isn't the most stable branch in the world.

"Woaaaaw!" You grab a tight hold as your weight tilts the upright branch significantly to the right. You lean the other way, only to find that this overbalances it. It tilts way over to the left, with you hanging on for dear life.

"Hey, that looks like fun!" Dave calls from his tree. "I'm coming over!"

"What?"

"What are you guys doing?" Danielle wants to know. Soon both Dave and Danielle are climbing up into your tree.

"You guys, I don't think this branch is strong enough to hold three people...."

"Of course it is," says Dave, seating himself just below you. A gust of wind sends the branch tilting again. When Danielle gets on, it tilts even more, like an airplane swooping in flight.

"Out of my way!" Dave announces. "This is a pilot's job!"

You make way as he seats himself at the highest point possible, grabbing two smaller, leafy branches for controls. "Good evening, guests. This is your captain speaking. As you may or may not know, we are going to be flying over some dangerous territory tonight: UFOs have been sighted, and a great deal of turbulence has been predicted. Fasten your seat belts, hang onto your hats, and away we go. Wings, check. Cabin." He looks back at the two of you. "Check. Fuel, check."

"Dave, can't we just skip the preflight checks and get going?" Danielle asks.

"Don't you know that the preflight check is one of the most important parts of a pilot's job?" Dave asks. "Flaps, check." You and Danielle sit patiently for the rest of the preflight check and then wait while Dave revs up the engine and taxis down the runway.

He leans back for the takeoff. Because of the nature of the branch, you really are looking up into the sky. "Uh, oh, it's a meteor shower! Everybody lean right!" You lean right. The branch leans dangerously, creaking as it goes. "Left!" You lean left. You battle everything from an erupting volcano to enemy fighter jets. When a fighter jet shoots off one of your plane's wings and you all lean forward to simulate a crash, it is rather terrifying. Then Dave resigns as pilot and you and Danielle each take a turn.

A cracking noise at the base of the branch ends the game. Besides, it's getting late. You each eat one mango sitting up in the tree, juice dribbling everywhere. Then you pick eight mangoes each and trudge back up the mountain to Kahunda Rock. By the time you get back to your bicycles, you are all exhausted. The trip down the long hill is relaxing. You don't have to pedal at all but coast down the hill at breakneck speeds until you hit the sandy road at the bottom and gradually slow down. Needless to say, you all lose several mangoes off your bike racks in the process. Dave loses his hat halfway and has to stop.

The story of this trip actually ends about a month later. You left Africa with the beginnings of five boils on your back. At least they look like boils, but they itch horribly.

You get an email message from Aunt Debbie:

"We have discovered a new kind of parasite, called mango worms. The dog and both the kids have had them. They make bumps that look

like infected bug bites or boils, each of which houses a small white grub. If you have anything like this, you should deal with them immediately.

The biggest one that we found so far was on the dog's back in a sack of fluid. It was a white grub about three-fourths of an inch long. We've found that the best way to treat these grubs is to put Vaseline over the breathing hole on each of the 'boils' and cover it with a Band-Aid overnight. The grubs are dead by the next morning and should pop right out when you squeeze the fluid sack. Use a needle to fish them out if necessary."

At first when you see the five dead white grubs *outside* your body, you feel immense relief! You don't itch anymore. But later, when you begin to think about the fact that you had maggots living in your back for over a month, it's absolutely disgusting! They *are* your most unique souvenirs of Africa.

THE END

"Come on!" you shout to Dave and Danielle as you run for the tiny house. You wonder whose house it is. Surely they'll understand. You reach for the handmade wooden handle and pull. The door opens. Dave and all the African children follow you inside. You quickly shut the door. The light from the crack under the door is the only light entering the building. This is good, because it also means that the bees can't get in any other way. You stomp on a couple of bees that work their way under the door. For the time being, you are safe.

"What is this place?" Danielle asks through the darkness.

"There's a type of a bed on this side," Dave replies.

A couple of the older boys have joined you at the door to stomp on any winged intruders. You can still hear the bees outside. Your eyes gradually adjust to the darkness. A couple of the children appear to have been stung but no more than that.

"Good thinking," Dave commends you through the darkness. "Though I've gotta say that when I saw you run into someone's house without knocking, I was a little surprised."

"How long do you think we'll have to wait before the bees calm down?" Danielle asks.

"I don't know," you respond.

"It was pretty good thinking, running in here to get out of the bees," Danielle affirms.

You can't help but feel pleased with yourself, being a newcomer and all.

Dave's watch lights up in the dark so you are able to keep track of the time. After 15 minutes, when no bees are coming in anymore, you cautiously open the door and peer out. Then everyone rushes out as quickly as possible.

You get to the wedding reception and are shown to seats near Uncle Darryl and Aunt Debbie. All the seats are set up in the courtyard of the bride's family homestead. Right now people are giving cash gifts to the bride and groom. A man at the front calls guests by name and loudly announces how much they gave. The bride's grandmother, obviously very drunk, is making a spectacle of herself, shouting and sometimes dancing during the proceedings.

After the money has been collected, other gifts are presented. The family gives *kangas* and dishes. The kitchen crew presents a great deal of cookware. Then it is time for the meal. The cake comes first. As two of the young women in the family dance out with the cakes, Aunt Debbie gasps. Two thick, crocheted afghans have been laid over the tops of the plastic bags, crushing her lettering. "Don't worry, Mom. At least it'll still taste the same," Dave reassures her. You get a small piece of the green cake. It tastes fine, except for the aroma of the bug spray that someone sprayed all over the cake bag to kill or to safeguard against ants, you're not sure which.

Dinner is excellent. The family has killed a cow and many chickens. The local fishermen have also been busy. Your table has large platters of rice and *ugali*, a thick starchy glob of cooked cornmeal. The meat sits in small bowls with broth. Another young woman comes around with a pitcher of water, which she pours over your hands into a basin. There is no soap, but the water is scalding hot, sterilizing your hands completely. Dave and Danielle are busy demonstrating to you how to eat *ugali* with your fingers.

"Make sure you only eat with your right hand," Danielle cautions. "Eating with your left hand is unacceptable."

"It's the *toilet* hand!" Dave whispers to you and smothers his laughter. Danielle gives her brother a disgusted look. "Well, it is." Dave goes back to eating, looking pleased with himself.

"The other rule is: never double-dip into the sauce bowl," Danielle tells you.

"Also," Uncle Darryl leans over to join in the conversation, "when you eat a fish, never start at the head. Always start at the tail."

"How long did it take you guys to learn all this?" you want to know.

"As long as we've been here," Danielle answers.

"We learn a bit here and there," Aunt Debbie says. "It's amazing how many social conventions and taboos there are. But, if you think about it, we have just as many in our culture. Don't burp in public, maintain people's personal space, cover your mouth when you cough...."

The sodas have arrived. You, Dave, and Danielle are given orange Fantas. The adults got Cokes. One of your hostesses, noticing that you are seated a long way from either of the meat dishes, gives you your own bowl and pours some meat broth into it. She randomly selects a piece of beef and a piece of chicken to place in your bowl. You attempt to thank her and she understands, smiling. When you look down at the pieces of meat, however, a new problem presents itself. Your piece of chicken is three-lobed and very gray, quite different from the other, more traditional, pieces in the chicken dish. The oddly shaped piece of beefsteak looks quite good; all that concerns you is the three small hairs bristling out from it. You are hungry and it smells good. You're not sure how it would go over for you to put the meat back.

(If you eat the grayish piece of chicken meat, go to page 155.)
(If you eat the hairy beef, go to page 156.)
(If you decide not to eat either, go to page 158.)

You and Dave step between women selling bananas. You head for the sugarcane on the lower left-hand side of the market. You walk through the jewelry section. Three men with very elaborately painted fingernails are selling the necklaces, earrings and bracelets that are safety-pinned to the inside of their baskets. One man has a box of rings. About half of the rings have various letters of the alphabet on them, though only about a third of the letters of the alphabet are represented there. You see the first letter of your name on one of the gold rings as you walk through.

(If you want to buy the ring, go to page 95.)
(If you keep going, go to page 137.)

"Right!" you decide. You and Danielle head for the top part of the market first, the women's section. There are *kangas* everywhere.

"See if you can find me a blue or green one," Danielle requests. "Purple or yellow would be fine too. But try not to get one with a big pineapple or heart in the middle. They look weird when you wear them." You and Danielle divide and conquer. The *kangas* are folded and displayed in overlapping rows on tarps spread on the ground. You walk up to the first seller. The first thing you notice is his shirt, featuring a white woman in a swimming suit. He quickly pulls up his shirt to hide the woman, laughing as he realizes that in doing so he exposed more than he had intended. He then proceeds to show you *kangas*. You see Danielle down the way, looking at a red *kanga* with black half-moons all over it inside the border. You notice that all *kangas* have a message at the bottom written in Kiswahili. The man pulls out a yellow *kanga* and displays it for you. Yellow and orange stripes go horizontally across it, inside a thick, intricately designed yellow and orange rectangular border. The middle of the *kanga* features a large object, not a pineapple but...

"...a chicken!" Danielle appears happily at your side, takes the corners of the *kanga* and reads the Kiswahili writing at the bottom. "'*Napenda wageni.*' 'I love visitors.' Hmmm. Well, that's true most of the time." The seller has already pulled out another of the same design but in purple and green.

"No, I think I'll take the yellow one." Danielle begins to negotiate the price. She ends up paying 1,500 shillings for it.

You head farther down the market. This must be the miscellaneous section. The seller's tarps are covered with toothpaste, notebooks, soap, safety pins, string, D-cell batteries and pocketknives. Danielle kneels by one tarp and picks up the handmade pocketknives, examining each. "I need a new pocketknife," she explains.

One of the first things you notice, next to the Bic pens, nail clippers and toothpaste, are long sticks of yellow soap. They are the width and thickness of bars of soap, but five times as long. Danielle sees you looking at them. "Those are all-purpose soap; dish soap and laundry soap mostly...." Her voice suddenly trails off as she looks from the soap to the

African-made pocketknives. Her eyes brighten. She turns around and begins to negotiate with the seller. "Could you lend me 3,000 shillings?" she asks you. "I have a great idea!" You hand her your 5,000-shilling bill. She hands it to the seller whose eyes grow wide. He gets up and begins negotiating with his neighboring sellers to borrow enough money to change a 5,000. He returns with two 500s and a 1,000.

Danielle picks up her second purchase: six sticks of soap. She hands three of them to you and then proceeds to purchase a pocketknife for herself. "You might want to get a pocketknife too," she suggests. "If we're going to do soap carving, you may as well have your own knife." You hand over one of your 500s, finally understanding what is going on. You and Danielle select another knife from among the hand-crafted folding blades in a pile on the tarp. You choose a sharp, well-formed blade that opens and closes easily. By now a crowd has gathered, watching you and Danielle in solemn silence. Dave works his way through the large crowd, an 8-foot stalk of sugarcane slung over one shoulder. You and Danielle stand up, finished.

"Danny!" Dave gawks along with the rest of the onlookers. "How could you possibly use all that soap?"

"Oh. These two are for you." Danielle hands him two of the six 2-foot bars of soap, one from her, and one from the top of your stack. "Two are for you, two are for me, and two are for our guest. You're right, it *would* take me a very long time to use six sticks (that is, 30 individual bars of soap) all by myself."

"I'll say," Dave agrees, looking at the four feet of soap he is holding. He follows his sister through the crowd, still mystified. You decide to help him out.

"She's planning to do soap carving," you tell Dave.

"Ahhhhh!" Suddenly all is clear. Then Dave wrinkles his forehead. "Sounds like a bit of a waste. Of soap, I mean." You are all heading down the market road to the lake.

"Not really," Danielle argues. "We can keep our carvings forever!"

"At least we can wash our hands with them someday; what about the shavings?" Dave wants to know.

"We can put them in the blender with some water and make liquid soap for the bathroom," Danielle says happily. "I read about it in the *Good Housekeeping* magazine someone sent us in a box."

"Soap in the blender? Bleh!" Dave spits on the ground.

"Gross, Dave!" Danielle was not impressed by his gesture.

"Everyone here spits on the ground all the time! Besides, who's talking about *gross*? The blender will never be the same again."

"I think it'll be worth it," Danielle decides, "even though we *will* have to use the generator to power it."

When you get home, you all set up your materials. Danielle clears a place on her desk for you to work. The desk is made of plywood, sanded but not varnished, so cut marks won't show. Dave sits down on the floor and sets to carving. Danielle's first order of business is a curly snake. She sets it aside, preferring to make a dolphin. Dave carves his name.

By the time Uncle Darryl and Aunt Debbie get home that evening, a soap nativity set, complete with Mary, Joseph, the baby Jesus, and a donkey/cow (you can't really tell which it's supposed to be) are on their way to completion. Danielle's snake breaks when it falls on the floor, and she debates whether or not softening the two sides with water will work to mend it. You may be amateur carvers now, but time will tell whether you stay that way.

The End

You decide to keep the story of the animal to yourself. After all, what good would it do to tell anyone something so unrealistic? You still wonder. When you get back to your home country, you search encyclopedias and the Internet looking for any record of an animal similar the one you saw, but you can't find anything. Did you discover a new species? What was it you *really* saw? You'll never know.

THE END

"Kites sound good," you tell Dave and Danielle. You've seen enough bugs for one day. You and Danielle follow Dave into his room, where he gets the book off the shelves.

"We got this kite book in a missionary box from a church," Dave tells you, sitting down on his bed. "We get packages every once in a while. The last box had M&Ms in it!" He smiles, savoring the memory. You and Danielle lean over the book, one on each side of Dave. "The only problem with making something," Dave interjects, "is that there aren't any craft stores around here."

"We'll have to improvise. What are we going to do about kite string, Dave?"

"You remember when I bought those three rolls of fishing line on our last bike ride?"

"So, you were planning for this all along?" She smiles.

"Yup."

You all skip the knot-tying section of the book and look at the kites.

"The Eddy kite is supposed to be really stable," Dave suggests.

"It doesn't look very exciting." Danielle looks at it skeptically.

"How strong do you think that the wind is right now?" Dave asks. "The Bird Kite needs a wind force of about 2–5 on a wind range scale of 1–6."

"It's probably about a 3 or a 4," you decide, looking out of the window at the swaying trees.

"Do we have any 'flexible plastic tubing?'" Dave asks Danielle.

"You mean like drinking straws?"

"Sounds good enough."

You decide to build the Bird Kite, Danielle the Japanese Fighting Kite. Dave decides that the Box Kite would be a worthy challenge.

"We don't have any wooden dowels, do we?" Dave asks.

"No, you need a hardware store for that," Danielle says regretfully. Dave lends you a pocketknife, and you all go out into the yard looking for straight sticks. You, in particular, look for flexible *green* sticks. The "wings" of your Bird Kite are supposed to flap as the kite goes up, which means that the middle stick, "the spar," needs to be particularly strong and flexible. Dave finally points you toward the type of tree from which he always gets sticks for bows and arrows.

"Sometime later, before you go, we can make bows and arrows and have an archery contest!" Dave suggests.

Dave stays quite a bit longer out in the yard cutting sticks. The Box Kite takes eight lengths of sticks rather than the two that your kite and Danielle's take.

Besides the sticks, you use a black plastic garbage bag and some packing tape. You and Danielle share one bag; after all, they aren't available less than an 18-hour drive away, and you want to conserve them. You finish your kite first and spend the last ten minutes carving the sticks and adding bits of tape to make sure that your kite is perfectly balanced. Danielle makes two tassels for hers, according to the directions. She ties them onto the corners of her kite. The two of you raid the ragbag and cut long strips of cloth from an old stained pillowcase. You each tie the fabric strips end to end and attach them to your kites.

Danielle agrees to help you launch your kite first. As she runs away from you, carrying your kite above her head, you can feel the wind's pull. "Avoid the trees!" she calls as she throws the kite up into the wind. Your kite loops once, wings flapping wildly, and dives into the sand. You wind up the string and then try to launch Danielle's kite. Hers loops violently around four times before crashing, tassels swaying.

You and Danielle decide that your kites need longer tails to stabilize them and add more strips of fabric.

You try your kite again. It goes up at once, then dives into an African neighbor's yard full of trees. You and Danielle go to retrieve the kite and greet the family. One of the children, a boy named Daudi, helps you as you painstakingly retrieve the kite with all its string. After adding seven long strips of fabric, your kite darts side to side but doesn't loop. You pull at the string as your kite rises higher and higher, its bird's wings flapping. It keeps going up. Soon your kite is unbelievably high and basically flying itself. The young neighbor boy is helping Danielle get her kite up. Her kite is only half as big as yours. She has added no fewer than nine strips of cloth and so far the Japanese Fighting Kite's violent nature is only slightly dampened. She is adding three more strings when Dave arrives.

"Danny, what are you *doing*?" Dave asks as he comes out with his completed Box Kite.

"My kite won't behave, so I'm adding more tail. Impressive kite!" Danielle comments, looking at his Box Kite and then going back to her work.

"Thanks," Dave acknowledges her compliment but is still confused as to why she is adding more cloth. "Since when does a kite only a foot wide need a 24-foot tail?"

"This one does! It's a war kite, remember?" Danielle hands the kite to Daudi who runs with it, Danielle unwinding the string.

"If I had to guess, it's probably that tail that's keeping it from behaving," Dave decides. Then Dave notices you and the kite string in your hand. He looks up, and then way up to where your kite is flying, and gasps. "Wow!"

Danielle's kite loops once weakly and noses into the ground more gently. "Two more strips oughta do it," she decides.

Jerking from side to side with its newly lengthened tail, Danielle's kite lifts off from the ground. This time it works. Looking like an agitated woman wearing earrings, the kite works its way up into the sky, higher and higher.

"You guys, now that your kites are working, I was wondering if we could take our kites down to the point," Dave suggests. "That's the sand peninsula where the fishermen fish. We could fly them out over the lake."

This sounds good to you and Danielle, so you all head down to the lake.

The fishermen stare as the three of you and Daudi approach with your odd creations. They have never seen a kite before. They laugh uproariously when you first try to launch your kites into the air, but their laughter turns to awe as the tiny kites with the long weighted tails pull away, up into the sky, yours flapping its wings and Danielle's jerking from side to side. Dave has to go back to get some tape. When a Box Kite crashes, it requires repairs. Finally all three kites are up! They must be at least a mile from shore, and you have no idea of their altitude. High-flying lake birds are flapping around them curiously. Daudi takes a turn flying each kite occasionally so one of you can sit down.

"I wonder if Mom and Dad can see our kites from the wedding," Danielle muses. Daudi is flying her kite now.

"Probably, *if* they happen to look up!" Dave decides. All in all, you are pretty proud of yourselves.

When you hear the first peal of thunder, you all start reeling in your creations. Remembering Benjamin Franklin's experiment with a kite and lightning, Danielle suggests that you abandon your kites all together, but you and Dave won't stand for it. You worked hard on those kites! In the end, you each reel in your kite.

The wind has probably reached a 6 on the wind range scale. Your clothes whip around you as you watch a storm begin over the water. As far as the eye can see, the waves are coming. The rumble resounding through the air is deafening. The birds that were flying curiously around your kites are finding it difficult to maintain control. You pick up a few stray feathers on the way back to the house, including one feather that is as long as your elbow to your fingertips. It probably originated with one of the enormous marabou storks standing unperturbed on the beach when the storm hit. The fishermen were gathering in the fishing hut when you decided to go home.

When Uncle Darryl and Aunt Debbie get home, you have a lot to tell them. They listen to your descriptions of how high up and far away your kites flew. They are even more impressed when they see it for themselves the next day.

THE END

You pass the jewelry section and head over to the sugarcane. The sugarcane stalks lean over a long, thin board pounded into two small market trees. Children are standing around, many ripping fibrous strands off 6-inch pieces of sugarcane with their teeth and chewing them. The ground is littered with the white remains of cane sucked clean of all its juice. Dave is thinking aloud. "Hmm, let's see. If Danny and you and I each eat three sections, that's nine. And Dad will want one too, so that's ten...." Sugarcane looks just like bamboo. It is encased in a hard wooden peel on the outside. Like bamboo, it grows in sections.

"*Labda hi*," Dave is negotiating with the seller. By now a crowd of about 30 people have gathered to watch your purchase.

"*Shilingi saba*," the man compromises.

"*Saba? Sawa*," Dave sorts through the change in his hand. "Ten times 7 is 70, so I need a 50 and a 20...."

"He's cheating you, Dave," Danielle says, suddenly behind you.

"I know." Dave looks up. "But think of it this way. A dollar is equal to around 700 Tanzanian shillings. I'm paying 10 cents for all of this sugarcane. I should be paying only around 7 cents, but is the 3 cents a big enough deal to fight over?"

"You'll get a reputation as a pushover," Danielle reminds him.

"This time I don't care." Dave pays for the sugarcane. Danielle sighs.

"So how did your shopping go?" Dave asks Danielle as he shoulders the cane and you all weave your way through the crowd and out of the market. The market is in the process of completely closing down. As you walk down the wide market path toward the lake, you see the wooden island ferries preparing to leave.

"I didn't find a *kanga*," Danielle answers. "I was nervous and decided to come back and join you guys."

"Why were you nervous?"

"Some men were sitting around making kissing noises at me." Danielle blushes miserably.

"Next time I'll go with you," Dave reassures her. Danielle perks up considerably after that.

You are walking in front of the fishing camp. You glance out at the lake and see a strange sight.

Far out over the water, something like a long black funnel is spiraling out of the clouds. Looking like a black tornado, it is circling over the water far out in the bay. The thing is obviously gigantic!

"You guys!" You point at the swirling mass of cloud that is getting lower and lower.

"A tornado?" Danielle is standing in shock.

Dave's mouth is hanging open. He suddenly snaps back to life. "Come on, guys, we have to get home!"

"But we don't have tornadoes here!" Danielle is running down the path behind you. Dave, with his piece of cane, is running ahead. You pass the men's bathing area and then look out at the funnel cloud. It has reached the lake surface and is sucking water up into the clouds. You keep running. You all stagger up the sandbank and run toward the house. Simba runs out barking.

"Mom, Da-ad!" Dave yells. "Wait, they're not here! They went to the wedding!"

"You guys! It's okay!" Danielle calls from the back of the line. "The tornado is dissipating!"

"What?" You and Dave turn around. Sure enough, the funnel cloud is getting weaker. The three of you watch it as it disappears into the clouds.

"We need to keep an eye out for another one, though," Dave reasons.

"But those must be pretty unusual, or we would have seen one before." Danielle sits down weakly. "I wonder if fish have been sucked up into the clouds. Wouldn't that be awful? I guess there are worse ways to die."

"Yeah." Dave smiles in wonderment. "What if it rains fish? That'd be cool! They'd probably be frozen; after all, it's cold up there in the atmosphere...."

"Dave!" Danielle protests.

The funnel cloud dissolves as it slowly pulls back up into the sky. Danielle gets up to go inside. "You guys better come inside, too. You wouldn't want to be hit by a frozen fish."

When Uncle Darryl and Aunt Debbie come back, the three of you have quite a story to tell them. Uncle Darryl tells you that the funnel cloud was probably a waterspout. Heat rises, so the right amount of cold air over warm water will actually encourage the warm water to rise while the cold air sinks down, creating a spiraling waterspout. You are just glad you got to see it. You read later that in unusual circumstances, a waterspout can turn into a full-fledged tornado and come onto land. You're glad that didn't happen.

THE END

Having decided to play War, you crawl through the brush at the edge of the yard, sweating in the dust as the faint sound of voices lures you on. The rules in this game are simple. If anyone spots a member of the other team and shouts "Bang," while pointing a bent stick (a gun) in their direction, the other team member has to fall down on the ground for the count of 50 (though, as you've observed, some people seem to count much faster than others).

When you, Dave and Danielle discussed the game at the beginning, you had several choices of which kind of War to play. Captain War means that each team designates one member of their team as the captain. This person has the benefit of being able to give orders that must be obeyed; however, if the captain is captured by the other team and taken over to his or her enemy's territory, he or she must "fess up" to their identity, at which point that captain's team loses. Flag War simply means that the opposing team must gain possession of the other team's flag. This idea was discounted because last time they played it, one team buried their flag, making it impossible to find. Fort War occurs when each team is issued a red handkerchief that they are required to place in a visible location within their most secret fort. When the other team finds the fort, the war ends. You all have decided to play Conqueror War, a combination of Captain and Fort. When the designated captain, (unknown to the other team) sets foot in and "conquers" the other team's secret fort, marked by a red handkerchief, the game ends. Danielle explained the game to the African children. It took a while because she didn't know several words, like the verb "to fall down," but Dave was willing to demonstrate. The difference between Captain War and Conqueror War is that in Captain War, the captain has to reveal his or her identity when captured. In Conqueror War, the prisoners don't have to tell if they are the captain or not.

When it came time to play, the girls all wanted to stay together with Danielle, and one of the boys stayed with his older sister. Dave wanted you on his team. "Danny's Kiswahili isn't perfect and mine is even *worse*," he explained. "I want someone on my team I can plan with! That's how you win."

You, Dave, and the four African boys playing on your team have already chosen your fort. Facing Lake

Victoria, your territory is the right side of the yard. The house marks the boundary. One of the boys wanted to put the flag in the storeroom since it *is* on your territory, but you and Dave agreed that this would be too obvious. Your whole team debated putting it in the brush or down by the lakeshore. Then you came up with the idea universally declared the best. Your flag is hidden up in a tree *on the other team's land!* The flag is not visible unless you stand directly under the tree and look up. The other team will be poking around on your land looking for your fort, so chances are they'll never find it. Two of the African boys have stayed behind on your territory to discover any invaders; the rest of you have nothing on *your* land to guard so you've begun your all-out attempt to seek out the other team's fort and to identify their captain. If you can capture their captain, they'll never be able to win, but if you can't find their fort, you'll never succeed either.

Dave is your team's captain. He insisted, as he is the only one who can speak both English and Kiswahili. You think that he was too obvious a choice for captain because the other team will figure it out, but everyone went along with it. He also wanted to spy, but everyone agreed that would be too dangerous. He needs to stay hidden until he can safely penetrate the fort, once the rest of you discover it.

You crawl forward, listening to what is mainly Danielle's voice. The girls are discussing something, and you hear your name mentioned. Since there are only three of them, you conclude that their other two team members must have gone off to spy and look for your team's fort.

You hear "Bang, Bang!" shouted way off to the left. Three of the girls run off to investigate, leaving Danielle behind in the clearing. Now would be an ideal time to take a hostage, but you haven't explored very far yet. Danielle may be the captain, but you want to find the fort before you arouse attention.

(If you try to take Danielle prisoner, go to page 173.)
(If you sneak off to keep exploring, go to page 175.)

You wait until you, Aunt Debbie, Dave and Danielle are all at the dinner table before telling them about the animal. Since Uncle Darryl was going to Sengerema, they decided to come home after the church service. No one felt like going back for the wedding reception and dinner.

As soon as Aunt Debbie finishes the prayer, you describe the large, hotdog-shaped mammal.

Danielle's eyes grow wider and wider. Dave watches her with a smirk; Aunt Debbie eyes you quizzically. "And it went after my chicken?" Danielle is shocked.

Dave can't hold it in anymore. He bursts into gales of laughter. "Danielle! Of all the things to be fooled by...a giant hotdog!"

Aunt Debbie cuts in. "Well," she nods to you, "you tell a good story! I could have *sworn* that you believed every word of what you were saying. You even had me fooled for a minute."

"It's true!" you insist. But now even Danielle isn't sure.

"There's only one way to find out for certain," Aunt Debbie states decisively.

"How?" you ask.

"We'll ask our night guard!" Aunt Debbie declares. "He's bound to know about all of the wild animals around here. He can tell us if what you're describing really exists. It'll be really incredible if it does!"

"A new species!" Dave says with true excitement. Then, remembering that he hasn't been fooled, he goes back to eating.

"You said that Simba chased it out of the yard without barking?" Danielle asks.

"Yeah," you confirm.

"She only does that when she's going to kill something." Danielle looks skeptical and a bit frightened. You don't know what to think.

That night Aunt Debbie asked the night guard about the strange animal, giving the bizarre description that you did. He recognizes it immediately, "Oh, yes, *that* animal," and then gives her an explanation in Kiswahili that she later relays to you in English.

"'Normally it survives on its own in the wild. Its interactions with people are usually just the times that it goes after their chickens. Also,' the night guard said, 'it is an extremely *fierce* animal. It can take on two dogs and win.'"

"Probably because of its huge teeth," Dave decides. "That thing could probably swallow a chicken whole!"

"So that's why Simba decided to leave it alone after she had chased it out of the yard!" Danielle adds. "Simba is a big, powerful dog, but I guess she met her match."

"This is when I like being a missionary kid in a foreign country," Dave sighs happily. "We now know of a large fierce animal species that has eluded zoos in Western countries for centuries!"

"What shall we call it?" Danielle asks thoughtfully.

"It already has a name in Kisukuma," Aunt Debbie reminds you all.

"But we need to give it a name in *English*," Danielle insists.

"Hey, I saw it first!" You should have first dibs on the animal, after all.

"So what will *you* call it?" Danielle asks again.

"The Phantom of the Hotdog!" Dave suggests proudly. Danielle giggles. Despite all of the other names you come up with, that's the one that sticks.

THE END

Whatever the man is trying to get across to you must be very important. You quickly glance around to check if there is any danger of a wild animal attacking you or a tree branch falling on your head. There doesn't seem to be. You're not really sure what he's trying to say. The man is now walking toward you. Speaking in another language, he starts explaining something to you rapidly. Then, when he gets to you, to help you understand completely, he reaches down, picks up a twig, and draws an almost imperceptible line in the wet cement of the steps. You understand. If you had gone any farther, you would have left a permanent mark on Neema's family's new home. Seeing that you understand, the man smiles and goes back to his work. You run around the back of the foundation, scare the goat off and chase it over to Neema's house. As soon as the goat sees Neema, it runs up and follows her like a little dog. When you all finally sit down to play games, it tries relentlessly to climb into her lap. She explains, through Danielle, that her family took this little goat from a tiny uninhabited island out on the lake. Neema took care of it in its younger days, so it thinks she is its mother.

As you play, Neema's 4-year-old sister is taking a bath in a basin set out in the yard. She continually sends her 2-year-old sister to fetch things for her, such as soap, a washcloth and clean clothes. There are more distractions as you play cards. Danielle's cat Chiro arrives. Apparently she followed the two of you to Neema's house. Danielle and Neema immediately put her to work at one of her favorite pastimes: hunting rats around Neema's family's food stores. A rat's jawbone left on the floor of the kitchen tells the story of Chiro's escapades. A man stops by and asks for a drink of water. Despite the fact that Neema is busy, it is her job to get it for him.

You find out why Danielle and Neema like Old Maid. After playing so much, they can often guess which card each of them will take from the other player's hand. They relentlessly try to fool each other. When Danielle declares that it's time to leave, you are halfway through a game of Slapjack. You finish the game and then, after saying good-bye to everyone in the family, hurriedly take your leave, knowing that you'll be late. Neema walks you to the edge of the property, as is traditionally done with visitors. You feel exhausted as you walk home. There are few things more tiring than a cross-cultural experience, no matter how much fun it is.

THE END

As you lead Danielle away, the triumphal shouts of the girls under the tree inform you that you were wrong. The true captain, Lydia, is up in the tree with the red handkerchief in her hands. Later, when the children go home, Dave and Danielle are already planning their next game. Not War, but something quieter and just as difficult.

"A treasure hunt!" Danielle informs you excitedly.

"But *not* the game with all the notes that you have to find one after the other," Dave clarifies for you.

"No, with actual maps," Danielle explains. "Buried treasure! We could bury it way out in the brush and make maps for each other, marking out real landmarks like weird-looking trees, odd piles of rocks, stick arrangements...."

"We'll probably have to set up the rocks and the sticks ourselves," Dave decides.

It's clear that your adventures in Eastern Africa have only just begun.

THE END

The chicken actually tastes pretty good, as long as you don't look at it. "You got the gizzard!" Danielle laments. It's obviously one of her favorite chicken pieces. You give her a part and keep eating.

Dave stares at the piece of beef in your bowl for several minutes. "It just reminds me of a...naw, couldn't be!" He goes back to eating.

(Go to page 158.)

The piece of beef is crunchier than you expected. It is also salty and quite flavorful. Not bad. Dave looks over and nods respectfully. "So, how do you like the nose?" You stop in mid-bite. Danielle's jaw drops. You look down at your piece of meat. Those three hairs poking up between those sections must be the nostrils. There is no doubt.

"Can I have a taste?" Dave pleads. "I just want to be able to say that I've eaten one."

"Gross!" Danielle is not so enthusiastic.

"Don't worry." Dave grins. "Haven't you ever heard the 'Missionary Prayer?'" He recites it for your benefit:

> *Lord,*
> *Where you lead me I will follow,*
> *What you feed me I will swallow,*
> *But it's up to you, Lord True,*
> *To keep it down and pass it through.*

"Can I have some of your gizzard? That chicken piece in your bowl, right there." Danielle seems to have been distracted.

"Dad always adds a word to that prayer," Dave tells you. "He always says, 'To keep it down and pass it *sloooowly* through.' I guess he's eaten a few things that went through too fast!"

Aunt Debbie and Uncle Darryl farther down the table aren't doing so well with their beef. They got the small intestine and something else that they're keeping hidden at the bottom of the bowl. They revert to chicken for the rest of the meal.

(Go to page 158.)

You and the missionary family are given spoons to go with the rice. You observe, however, that many other people are eating it with their hands. You, Dave, and Danielle try eating it with your hands for a while and then give up.

After the meal you are each given a cup of *chai*, tea with milk and sugar already generously mixed in. You are terribly thirsty, but Dave and Danielle have warned you about the temperature of the tea. "It's scalding! Don't drink it now; wait!" Unable to stand your thirst anymore, you take a small sip, discover the truth and wait another ten minutes before trying again.

Now it's time for speeches. Each of the bride's and groom's male relatives and honored male guests give long speeches. It's beginning to get dark. After a while Uncle Darryl suggests that you three be allowed to go home, since the speeches aren't really for your benefit. You all couldn't agree more. Uncle Darryl gives you a house key, and you creep quietly out of the compound. Dave and Danielle are pretty sure that they'll be able to find their way home.

It's getting dark as you hurry down the dirt street. By the time you get to the top of the road leading down from the village, the signs of night are evident all around you. The sun is setting over the forest below, and crickets are chirping.

"Why didn't we think to bring a flashlight?" Dave asks as you walk along the edge of the forest to the beginning of the driveway.

"We don't need it," Danielle states confidently. Just then a cat runs across the road in front of you. A *big* cat. You all stop dead in your tracks.

"Was that what I think it was?" Dave asks.

"A bobcat," Danielle breathes. "And it looked like it was heading toward our house! They like chickens," she moans.

"We only have one, and she'll be fine!" Dave assures Danielle.

"How do you know?" Danielle isn't so certain.

"Simba's there, of course!" Dave says happily.

"Isn't she tied up?" Danielle reminds him.

"Oh...." Dave remembers. You all run home.

When you reach the yard, Danielle runs to the chicken house, peers inside to make sure Fryer Cluck is the only thing in there and then slams the door on the startled chicken. After circling the post a number of times, Simba is tied up to her neck. You and Dave unwind her and her leash from the post. You unlock the door and enter the darkened house. Dave switches on lights powered by large batteries charged by solar panels during the daytime. You're now free to spend the evening as you like, but you are too tired. It's been a long day.

THE END

You decide that you would rather stay on the ground. You walk around behind a tree to collect the two mangoes that Danielle dropped. "Aren't you going to climb?" Danielle calls down to you.

"I'd rather not." You stoop to pick up the fruit. Suddenly Dave yelps and drops from his tree. Unfazed by the 10-foot drop, he stands up, looking very excited.

"Are you okay, Dave?" Danielle calls down.

"Ouch! It's in my pant's leg!" Dave pinches whatever it is between his finger and thumb, crushes it and then shakes it out onto the ground. An unidentifiable black insect unfolds itself on a dry leaf on the ground and then crawls haphazardly toward Dave. It's a large ant and it isn't dead yet.

"Was that a jump or a fall?" Danielle asks, hurrying down from her tree.

"Sort of a combination of the two," Dave tells her. "My tree had *siafu* in it!"

"*Siafu*?" you ask.

"Army ants," Dave clarifies. "Ouch!" he yelps again. "There's one in my shirt!" He quickly pulls the shirt over his head and shakes it violently. Suddenly you feel a miniature but very painful bite on your thigh. You slap your hand on your leg, only to get bitten again. Then you feel another bite on your back. You look at the ground, and as it comes into focus, you realize that under the thousands of large dead mango leaves is a black sea of movement. Directly under where *you* are standing is what appears to be the highway of the ant metroplex, redirected up into your clothes.

Suddenly the expression "ants in your pants" has taken on a new meaning for you. You jump and slap at your legs, as you are bitten over and over.

"You're covered in them! You need to go strip!" Dave commands.

"Hurry!" Danielle shrieks.

You run out from under the mango trees into the tall rows of corn. At this point you are in too much pain to worry about someone seeing you. You rip off your clothes and begin swatting ants, many of which are clinging to your flesh. You throw off your socks and shoes too, getting bitten several times in the process. You never expected to be in this predicament—nude in a cornfield. You move over a couple of rows of corn to get away from the ants you've thrown off and start brushing the remaining ants out of your clothes, which are now inside out.

"Are you all right?"

"Do you need help?"

You hear the two voices from a short distance away.

"I'm fine. Don't come over here!" you shout back, suddenly a bit embarrassed. Maybe this is how Adam and Eve felt. You hurriedly brush off the remaining ants and shake your clothes thoroughly before putting them back on. Your skin stings from all the bites, making your clothes uncomfortable.

You head back over to Dave and Danielle who are waiting for you just outside the mango grove. "At least *your* tree didn't have any *siafu* in it," Dave is saying to Danielle.

"Besides, I think that our guest got bitten the most," Danielle says. They see you.

"Are you all right?" Danielle asks.

"I'm sore. How come you guys didn't tell me that there are ants in Africa that bite pieces out of you?" you want to know.

"I guess it just slipped our minds. Ouch!" Dave grabs at his pants leg and runs into the cornfield.

Eventually the three of you walk back up to the rock, get your bikes and ride home. On the way back down the missionaries' driveway, Dave points out a nest of whispering ants. Their resemblance to *siafu* makes you queasy. These ants make a whispering noise when you stir them up. Dave claims that this variety is harmless—nothing like the *siafu* you just encountered. You listen politely to their angry whispering and then ride quickly away. You've had enough of ants for one day.

THE END

You rush into the brush, leaving a free and momentarily confused Danielle in the clearing. She runs toward the sound of girls shouting under your team's fort. You almost collide with a small boy. You're out of luck; he's the one boy with the girls' team. *Where's his sister?* you wonder. It's too late to try to find your team members; you've got to guard the fort yourself. You hear a battle of "Bang! Bang!" going on behind you and know that your teammates already discovered the trouble. By the time you reach the clearing, the war is over. Lydia, the other team's captain, is already up in the tree with the red handkerchief.

"Just when I was going to make up an entire communication code!" Dave regrets mournfully as you head back to the house. "A bark would be a sign that there was trouble. A meow would be a summons. A bird whistle would be...."

The children want to play with Dave and Danielle's bicycles. You, Dave and Danielle spend the rest of the day teaching the kids how to ride in the sand. It allows for a soft landing when people fall off, but it's harder to pedal. You don't have a choice of terrain. Dave and Danielle live on the lakeshore; sand is everywhere.

Tomorrow maybe you'll go bike riding in the village. Dave and Danielle have assured you that there are many interesting destinations there. You'll find out.

THE END

You need to get the goat. The goat has noticed you and is edging away. You run quickly toward it. As your foot touches the first step of the foundation, strong hands grab your upper arms, lift you backward and set you on the ground. You look behind to see the man who was yelling. He points to the step and you look down to see a shoeprint, *your* shoeprint, in the wet cement steps of the foundation. The man is speaking rapidly while waving at the blemish, probably saying, "Look what you did! Don't you know that shoeprints in wet cement are *permanent*?" He then shrugs his shoulders and walks away, as if to say, "Oh, well. These things happen." When Neema's dad asks the man a question as he returns to the house, he answers briefly. Neema's dad walks over to survey the damage. Soon everyone in the family has come over to look at the step. Neema's stepmother laughs when she sees it, but the others just stand in silence. You get Danielle to apologize in Kiswahili for you, but the situation is still mortifying. Neema seems the least concerned of everyone and still wants to play games. You are glad when Danielle cuts the visit short. After playing three card games, you say good-bye.

On the way home, you and Danielle pass a very old woman walking down the road from the other direction. Danielle walks up to greet her, and you follow, thinking that at least you'll be able to do one thing right! Danielle shakes hands with the woman and curtseys. The woman is delighted. She also seems quite happy when you greet her, responding with a garbled "*Marahaba*" as you offer your hand to her. She is missing several teeth. As you shake her hand, you suddenly realize that the woman is missing three fingers and half of her thumb and first finger as well.

"Do you know her?" you ask as you and Danielle continue on your way.

"No," Danielle replies, mystified. "I greeted her out of respect for her age, and because she was the only other person on the road with us. It was the right thing to do. I wonder why she was missing so many fingers. An accident, maybe?" You keep walking in silence. Suddenly Danielle groans. "Oh, no! What if she had leprosy? That makes people lose fingers!"

Leprosy! The word falls like a hunk of lead. "You mean people around here sometimes get leprosy?"

"Yeah. A lot of the beggars in Mwanza have it, so I'm sure that it's made it out here."

"Can we get it just from shaking her hand?" you wonder.

"I don't know; we'd better ask my mom. She's a nurse; she'll know," Danielle decides worriedly.

When you and Danielle get home, the first thing you do is wash your hands very thoroughly with soap and water, over and over. Next you get out an encyclopedia. You find out that only 5 percent of the world population can get the disease, and even then, it is one of the least contagious of all contagious diseases worldwide, but you're still not sure. When Aunt Debbie gets home, she puts Danielle's fears to rest. "*Children* of people with leprosy almost never get the disease, even though they eat the same food as their parents, etc. The chance that the two of you could get leprosy from shaking someone's hand is almost nonexistent!"

You still wonder. Today was a hard day, though you made at least one person happy.

THE END

"*Hizi ni nini?*" one of the boys asks. Since you joined the boys working on the Little House, you have been listening to an English lesson that has been going on for some time now. One of the boys is holding up a tool and asking for its name in English. Dave glances down briefly from where he is tying grass to the roof. "A *rake*," he answers.

"*Ahlakey!*" the boy repeats.

"No! I mean *hapana*," Dave corrects himself. "Rake. RAKE!"

"*Lakey!*" the boy repeats. Clearly, the *r* is one of those sounds that doesn't translate well between languages. The African boys are also ending every word with a vowel.

"*Kama mbwa!* Like a dog!" Dave translates for you. "R-r-r-r-r-rake! Gr-r-r-r-r-r-r-r!" Dave growls to give the boys an appreciation for the sound. Simba looks up.

"Er-r-r-r-r-r-rakey!" the boy growls back. The other boys explode with laughter.

"That's right! *Vizuri sana!*" Dave congratulates him, but the boy, subdued by the laughter of his peers, goes back to working on the house.

"It's just as hard for me to try to learn the African languages," Dave tells you. "Kiswahili, the national language of Tanzania, has several sounds that don't exist in English. A flipped *r*, for example. And take the language that my dad is working on translating—Kizinza. It's a tonal language! That means that speaking is almost like singing, with high-pitched and low-pitched sounds. If you say Kizinza words without the tone or pitch, the words become meaningless!"

"So how many languages do you speak?" you ask Dave.

"English and some Kiswahili," Dave tells you. "Since Kiswahili is the national language, just about everyone in Tanzania, the Wazinza people included, can speak it. That's why I'm trying to learn it."

"Is there a translated Bible in Kiswahili?" you want to know.

"Yup, three different versions," Dave tells you.

"So, if all the Wazinza people speak Kiswahili and Kiswahili is a written language *and* there are three translations of the Bible in Kiswahili, why did your parents have to come here to write the Wazinza language and translate the Bible into it?"

"It's like a German friend of ours who is fluent in Kiswahili once said: 'I can read and understand a

Kiswahili Bible, but I don't learn anything new.' I guess the Wazinza people feel the same way."

By the time the boys go home, the roof of the Little House is mended and the back wall is covered in grass. "Now all we need is a good rain to test our work!" Dave comments. You agree. Then again the spray from a garden hose will do just as well. You bring out the hose to test your work, but when Aunt Debbie and Uncle Darryl get home later and the water in the water tanks is exhausted halfway through Uncle Darryl's shower, you discover your mistake. That's when you, Dave and Danielle get your first instructions on how to turn on the generator to fill the water tanks with the well pump.

THE END

Abruptly Danielle stands up and whistles. She waits and whistles again. You are sure this must be some kind of signal and wait to see its result. Just then Simba bounds out of the bushes. She leaps around Danielle. "Atta girl!" Danielle exclaims pleasantly. "Now, Simba. Go find Dave!" Simba starts off into the brush, across the clearing from you. Danielle follows.

It's obvious that with Simba's nose at her service, Danielle can find Dave anywhere. "Bang!" you say as softly as possible. Danielle turns around, sees you and the bent stick in your hand, falls to the ground and begins to count to 50. She loses her place with a giggle as Simba jogs around confusedly and licks her face. You take Danielle's "gun" and firmly grasp her arm as she gets up. "You're coming with *me*."

"So much for that idea." Danielle looks sadly at Simba. "Oh, well. My team will rescue me."

"Especially if you're their captain!"

"Whoever said anything about *me* being captain?" Danielle looks at you innocently.

Through a gap in the bushes you spot two of Danielle's teammates sitting under a tree, *your* team's flag tree, taking a breather. They'd better not look up! They haven't seen the red handkerchief above them yet. Just then one of them looks up. Just like that. She stands up excitedly, leaping in the air and pointing to the tree. You know that she's seen the red marker. Both of the girls run off into the woods, presumably to find their captain. Danielle hasn't seen them. If their captain *is* Danielle, then you've got the situation well in hand. They can't win until they rescue her. But if Danielle isn't the captain, you'd do better to let her go and alert your team to defend your fort before it's too late!

(If you take Danielle as far away as possible, go to page 152.)
(If you let her go and try to alert your team, go to page 165.)

You creep away from Danielle. No one needs to know you are here. There is too much territory to explore, and you're not taking any chances. Danielle stays behind in the clearing. You hear her whistling a signal but don't know what it means.

You hear someone coming toward you; you raise your stick gun. It turns out to be Samsoni, one of the older boys on your team. He seems very excited. He motions for you to follow him. At the far end of the yard, he points to the missionaries' thatch storage pile. Bundles of grass have been placed on top of planks resting on bricks. You and Samsoni race across and hide behind the pile. You peer underneath the boards. Sure enough, down underneath the planks and piles of grass, laid neatly across the cool sand, is the opposing team's red handkerchief!

All that remains is to get your captain, Dave. The rules of Conqueror War state that the captain must penetrate the opposing team's fort to win the game. Once Dave crawls into the space under these boards, you'll win! Unless…you stop cold. Nestled next to a brick, two feet from the red handkerchief, are the coils of a small green snake. You jerk back and sign to Samsoni what you saw. He looks too and jumps away in fear. A safe distance away you share a glance, thinking the same thought in different languages. The other team's fort now has a safeguard that no one would dare tangle with—a snake! It's time to report to the chief. You crawl into the brush only to hear voices approaching from the enemy's direction. You recognize Danielle's and several of the other girls' voices.

"It won't be long now," Danielle is saying. But she was speaking English! That could only mean one thing.

A sing-songy "Are we there yet?" from Dave confirms your deepest fears. The verdict is clear and the situation is grim. Dave has been taken prisoner.

You and Samsoni watch from the edge of the clearing where members of the other team and Dave are assembled. Crouched in the itchy, tall grass you plot a plan of action. At least in Conqueror War, Dave doesn't have to reveal that he is the captain. Right now, he's offering to make Danielle's bed for a week if she'll release him.

Stop it, Dave! you think to yourself. *If you act like you're too important she might suspect who you are.*

Simba has also joined the party in the clearing. "And I'll feed Simba every day for the next...." Dave is saying.

Danielle interrupts. "Actually, Dave, there is *one* small thing that you can do for us if you want to be released, but I don't think that you will."

Anything! you think to yourself.

"Anything! I'll do anything!" Dave responds.

"Where is your fort?" Danielle asks. "Our scouts have searched all over your land, which wasn't very well protected, by the way...."

Right. Samsoni is looking at you for an indication of what this conversation between Dave and Danielle in English is about. You motion to him to wait.

"We can't find your red handkerchief," Danielle continues. "It's supposed to be visible. Did you put it in a fair location?"

"Oh, yes," Dave agrees, trying to contain the smirk on his face.

"Really, really, Dave? You look like you're hiding something." Danielle stares incredulously at his face.

"It's way off the ground." Dave bites his tongue too late.

"Concealed among leaves, I suppose?" Danielle continues.

"No, no! Perfectly visible!" Dave counters.

"Is there anything else you would like to tell us?"

"No." Dave sits mute.

He *could* lie. But it appears that Dave and Danielle don't lie to each other.

"As soon as you tell us where your fort is, we'll let you go."

"How do you know that my team hasn't already found your fort?" Dave counters. "They might be finding it as we speak!"

"No, your team hasn't found it yet. They couldn't possibly!" Danielle is confident.

Sure we could, you think to yourself.

"We've sent out scouts to find your captain," Danielle continues, "so that even if you do find it, acting upon your find will be impossible."

"You know who our captain is?" Dave blinks.

"*Our guest*, of course!" Danielle declares triumphantly. "Our guest is the only person that none of our scouts have spotted yet."

Maybe you could cause a distraction, allowing Dave to "escape." Samsoni stands up beside you. "Bang! Bang! Bang!" he shouts. Caught completely by surprise, Danielle and the other two girls fall to the ground. You can tell that they're counting quickly. You and Samsoni each take one of them hostage. Why didn't you think of this before?

"Dave!" you explain hurriedly, watching the girls on the ground. "We found their fort, but there was a snake by it...."

"What?" Dave is distracted as he leaves the clearing.

"A snake!" Danielle, still ten counts away from being alive, is shocked.

"So we don't know how you can enter it," you finish as Dave turns back to face you.

"*You're* the captain?" Danielle shrieks at Dave.

"Run, Dave!" you urge him. "Under the thatch pile!" Dave dashes off. "Don't get bitten!" you shout. "Bang!" You fire as Danielle is about to get up.

"What?" Dave shouts, running backward toward the thatch.

"Okay, time out!" Danielle stands up. "What was that about a snake...?"

"Bang! Bang!" shout the girls as they finish counting.

"There's a snake under the thatch pile!" you shout over the noise.

At this point Samsoni and one girl are arguing about who shot whom first while the other girl insists you're supposed to be dead. Danielle breaks through the chaos and races toward the grass.

"Dave!" she shouts. "Stop!"

Dave is standing by the thatch, holding the red handkerchief in his hand. "Dave, get away from there!

They said there was a snake!" Danielle runs up, red-faced.

"Yeah, there *was*, but that was three months ago before we moved the pile on planks. There isn't anymore. See, we won!" Dave waves the red handkerchief in Danielle's face. Danielle looks to you for an explanation.

"The snake was next to one of the bricks just a few minutes ago," you explain. "It was small and bright green." The group goes silent. Samsoni is explaining it to the African children in the Luo language.

"Looks like we were protected twice." Danielle cringes. "When we put it under there, and when Dave got it out."

"It could have been a grass snake," Dave argues. "They're harmless."

"Or a green mamba," Danielle argues back. "You never know."

You finish the day with Kool-Aid popsicles. The African children spit them out, unused to the burning cold. Samsoni is congratulated for having found the flag. It was a good day.

THE END

Now that you're all together again, you, Dave and Danielle leave the cement church and head down a path, following the straggling crowd walking in small groups through the village to the wedding reception. Dave and Danielle have been joined by a group of African children, most of them boys. As you walk, you hear a strange humming sound in the air. Bees! Suddenly the noise is all around you. One of the small boys cries out in pain. You have to get away from these bees now! You see only two possible escapes. You could try to outrun the swarm, or you could find shelter. A nearby house appears to be solid, with no windows and a wooden door that you could close behind you and the others after you got inside. But the door is closed; what if it's locked? Time is of the essence.

(If you try to run out of the swarm, go to page 113.)
(If you run for the house, go to page 118.)

"Let's not play War," you decide. You're not in the mood for a strategy game right now, especially not one called War. You join the girls and Danielle, who start off their afternoon playing with Danielle's stilts. These are 8-foot sticks of wood with one small foot platform nailed about 3 feet up. By holding the longer part of the sticks and standing on the platforms, you can walk around. The soft sand is hard to walk on since the stilts always sink into the ground. The advantage of the sand is that no one gets hurt when they fall off.

You and the girls move on to playing with Danielle's hula-hoop. Some of the boys came over to join you. Their way of playing with a hula-hoop isn't the typical way you've seen—spinning it around the waist. Their version *does* involve more people, though. While one person holds the hoop, the others run at it and try to jump over or through the hoop without touching it. Two of the boys can dive through it and somersault on the other side like real acrobats. It's harder than it looks, you discover.

When you and the girls start playing with Jenga blocks, trying to make as tall a block tower as you can without it falling over, the boys go back to working on the house. That's when you notice the two girls seated off to the side. Upon closer examination you see that the older one has a razor blade and appears to be shaving something off the other girl's hand. When you get closer to them, you see that she is cutting off warts. When the girl with the razor blade finishes slicing off all of the younger girls' warts, she calls over one of the other girls to undergo the same procedure. She cuts off the next girl's hand and arm warts with the same razor blade, blood flowing freely. When she motions you to come over, you decline. Warts or no warts, this isn't an activity you want to take part in.

When Aunt Debbie comes home later, she is shocked to hear about this method of wart treatment. "That could spread AIDS!" You suppose that it could. By the time you, Dave and Danielle have listened to Aunt Debbie's 20-minute lecture on the subject of AIDS, you *know* that it could. AIDS is a blood disease that affects the immune system and is passed from person to person through the exchange of bodily fluids. There are many ways that AIDS can be spread, and you just witnessed one of them.

The End

Glossary

arusi: a wedding

asante: thank you

chai: tea with milk

chandalawe: red dirt that can pack into a hard surface; people sometimes layer it on paths and roads

chapati: a soft, tortilla-like unleavened bread made with flour and oil

Chiro: night (Kizinza word **omuchiro**); also the name of the missionaries' cat

cho: bathroom/outhouse

daga: small fish, 1 to 3 inches long, eaten in large numbers

duka: a small African store. Items are purchased through a window in the front side of the store. Merchandise is displayed on the walls inside behind the seller.

hapana: no

jiko *(jee-koe)*: a small, hourglass-shaped oven filled with charcoal

kanga: a 3 by 5 foot piece of patterned multi-purpose fabric; usually very colorful, consisting of a border, an inside design and a short text message at the bottom

kench: a triangular wooden structure that supports a roof

kenge *(kain-gay)*: a monitor lizard

Kiswahili: the national language of Tanzania

Kisukuma: the language spoken by the Wasukuma tribe

Kizinza *(key-zin-zah)*: the language of the Wazinza people

marahaba: do it a few times

mboga: the protein part of the meal/the part of the meal other than the starch [Example: When a meal includes rice, chicken, beans and spinach, the chicken, beans and the spinach all fall into the category of *mboga*; the rice does not.]

mchicha: spinach greens

mganga: doctor

mji *(m-jee)*: homestead/houses and immediate yard of one family

Mzinza: a member of the tribal group Wazinza

nzuri: good

samahani: excuse me

sebule: all-purpose living and dining room

Sengerema: the nearest town to Kahunda with medical facilities. It is a 3.5 hour drive away in the dry season and 5.0 hours in the rainy season.

shamba: a farm, usually agricultural

shikamo: the local greeting from a younger to any older person; "I grab your feet."

shilingi: a shilling or shillings (money)

shilingi ngapi: How many shillings?

siafu: army ants

Simba: lion; also the name of the missionaries' dog

sisimizi: sugar ants

soko: an African marketplace

sufuria: aluminum cooking pot with rim

ugali: stiff porridge made with corn flour and/or cassava flour

utusemehe: pardon our offense

Wasukuma: the largest tribal group in Tanzania (approximately 2.5 million); Kahunda is a Wasukuma village

Wazinza: the tribal group that speaks the language Kizinza

Wazungu: Western people or white people

zawadi: gift

WHAT'S WYCLIFFE

The family you read about in this book may not be real, but they represent thousands of people who are a part of the Wycliffe team. What's Wycliffe? It's an organization of people from all over the world. What do they have in common? They all love God and value the Bible as God's Word. *And* they want everyone, everywhere, to know about God's love and be able to hear God's Word in their own language.

More than 6,800 languages are spoken in the world. Still about 3,000 language groups don't have the Bible in their language. That means hundreds of millions of people have no way to hear God speak their language! How can they learn about Him? How can they have churches that teach the Word of God?

A young man named Cameron Townsend asked those questions more than 70 years ago. He was trying to give Spanish Bibles to people in Central America and realized that many of the people didn't even understand Spanish. All those languages without a Bible! Townsend was determined to do something about it. Through prayer and partnership, he started a school (SIL) and a mission organization (Wycliffe) to train people to do Bible translation and help get God's Word to the whole world.

Today about 5,000 people from all over the world are a part of Wycliffe. Thousands of other people are involved, working in partnership so everyone can have God's Word in the language they understand best. A few years ago a lot of these partners met together and agreed to pursue Vision 2025. The goal of the Vision is to see Bible translation in progress for every language group that needs it by 2025.

It's a vision for all of God's people, young and old! People all over the world are praying and working together. Some people pray and give money to help fund Bible translation. Some help on short-term projects; others commit their whole lifetime. Whole churches are getting involved: youth groups, women's groups, retired people. There is something for everyone to do! Translators are needed, but you don't have to be a translator to help with Bible translation. There are teachers, computer specialists, graphic designers, office managers....

What's Wycliffe? It's people like you who want everyone to hear God's Word in the language they understand best! Learn more about how you can be involved by going to *www.wycliffe.org*.

About the Author and Illustrator

Tania Matthews started writing the *East African Adventures* when she was 13 years old. She grew up as a Wycliffe missionary kid in Tanzania, Africa, where her parents served as Bible translators. Storytelling and writing have always been her hobbies. At 7 years old she began dictating stories to her mother to write down. Later she created little illustrated books using cereal boxes for covers. Tania finished high school in Kenya and currently attends the University of Tennessee at Chattanooga.

Judy Rheberg is a retired art teacher living in northeastern Wisconsin with her husband Jim. They spend winters volunteering for Wycliffe Bible Translators in Orlando, Florida. Judy loves animals. She raised sheep to save money for college and once had 10 collie dogs and 20 barn cats as pets. But Judy's all-time favorite animal is the horse. Even after plenty of rough rides and getting bucked off a time or two, she continues to love grooming, riding, reading about and drawing horses of all kinds.